I0580836

Aurora Books, an imprint of Eco-Justice Press, L.L.C.

Aurora Books
www.ecojusticepress.com

A Previous Life: And Colleted Short Stories
By Jerome Vergamini

Library of Congress Control Number: 2025935805
ISBN 978-1-945432-69-9

A Previous Life

by Jerome Vergamini

Table of Contents

LAZARUS:

It's approaching three years since she died. It started about seven years ago when she had a heart attack and ended up with a triple bypass. I noticed after she recuperated, that she began to have difficulty with words, with recalling names of people and objects. I thought it might have been the anesthesia. Maybe so, but it gradually continued to become more pronounced. We made little jokes about it, but little by little, I could see that it was bothering her. We still made it out to enjoy life as much as we could. We continued to attend the monthly symphony, we went to the ballet, to plays at the local theater, and out to dinner with friends. By the time Covid hit about four years after her surgery, we were, for the most part, relatively confined to home. She began to have problems with balance and walking, and I found myself being her primary caregiver. I didn't mind. She had had her share of caretaking me as well, especially after my knee surgery. We were still able to have conversations, reminisce, watch television together, and just enjoy each other's company. About a year into Covid, she began to struggle with keeping up a conversation as well as with balance and falling. She was a big enough woman that it was hard to get her back to her feet. After several 911 calls, I was concerned enough about safety to investigate memory care facilities. I reluctantly made the decision, after another trip to the ER, to get her admitted to one. Because of Covid, my visiting time was limited, but I saw her every day. Conversation became more one-sided. She gradually stopped eating much of anything, and she was placed on Hospice status, which meant that I had much more leeway in being able to stay longer to visit. I carried a small book of humorous short stories and read them to her so she could have some laughs. We arranged for a violinist friend to come and play for her. Time caught up with her, and after spending several hours with her one day, I received a call from the facility that she had passed away.

Numerous feelings passed through me --- sadness, relief, loss, grief. I knew it was coming, but now it was here. I was a bit too numb to know just what I was feeling. I was relieved that she was at peace, but at the same time felt like I had lost an arm. I was emotionally exhausted. I realized that I was also relieved that the inevitable was over, but the loneliness had just started.

I knew I had to make funeral arrangements, but Covid was still in the picture. People at the Temple were kind enough to offer a sensitive and helpful woman to perform a ceremony at the funeral home and at the gravesite. Despite Covid, a lot of friends were able to make it to the ceremony. She had impacted a lot of people in addition to her family.

Our kids gave me comfort, but they had their own lives. I went back to an empty house. My dog was there. It gave me something to do. I felt like Lazarus before he woke from the dead. Would I wake up? Time splashed on like wading back and forth in the shallow end of a swimming pool. Afterwards there was time to focus on the emptiness. How long would it take for Lazarus to wake up? Rumor has it that even after being brought from beyond, Lazarus was never quite the same.

Friends help -- coffee with friends, dinner with friends, phone calls with friends. I made it a point to keep busy. I took the dog to the park and met people there. I finished a book and got it published. I took photos. I played poker with friends. The TV was turned on to make noise. Reading a good book helped. I could do that alone. Outings to various events like concerts, plays, and social events tended to emphasize my sense of isola-tion, so they happened less.

As soon as I sit in a quiet space, I am aware of the sense that Lazarus has not yet fully come out of his coma. There is an emp-tiness that comes with the loss of someone who's been a major part of your life for sixty years. Yet there is an awareness that life will go on. There are people who still need my presence in theirs. There is more to learn, so I continue to splash my way through the pool. Writing helps.

Why do I write? I do so to keep my feelings from muddling my brain. I need to keep my thoughts connected and making sense. I need to keep directing my purpose and not to be overwhelmed by feelings of absence. I am not alone in the world, and I need to continue to be a part of it. I think I can feel Lazarus stirring. I don't know yet whether he will be fully awake, but he is beginning to take some deep breaths.

A Previous Life
Chapter One: Initial Contact

He didn't often take evening appointments, but this woman had been trying to get in to see him for a couple of weeks, and he hated to keep people waiting that long. He had arranged for the initial paperwork and preliminaries to be done before the actual time of the visit. Her voice had sounded urgent when he finally reached her to arrange a special time after his usual hours, but neither she nor he wanted to go into detail until they met in person.

He arrived about twenty minutes before the seven o'clock time he had given her. He wanted to look over her paperwork and get writing materials, Kleenex, a small pitcher of water and a couple of glasses ready. She arrived at five to seven. She looked a bit older than the forty-eight in her paperwork. Her long hair was graying and wrapped into a bun, and she had a slight tremor, but her hazel eyes were very much alive. Her skin had seen its share of sun, but the wrinkles on her face betrayed a history of smiling. She was in a dark pant suit that seemed to fit her demeanor. She held out her hand and said, "I am Beulah Blanche. I used to take a lot of heat for my first name. People thought it was 'old-fashioned', and other kids teased me about it." Her grip was firm and business-like.

"As you know, I am Dr. John Tucci. My friends often just call me Tooch. I'm glad I was finally able to get you in."

The office was small, with a roll-top work desk and chair. Against the wall beside the desk was a good-sized bookshelf with several volumes of history, philosophy, science, classic novels, and even some books from the New York Times bestseller list. Two more comfortable-looking chairs were off to the side of the desk with a small side table. There was no couch. A license and a diploma were framed on the wall across the room. On another wall was a framed print of Monet's water lilies.

He pointed to the comfortable-looking chair near his desk, and she sat down. He sat in the other chair near her.

"How can I be of help?"

She started right in.

"I was never a very pretty girl, so I married young when the opportunity came up. I was never really infatuated with him, but we had twenty-five decent years together and raised two daughters. My husband, John, died about a year ago of a heart attack. My daughters continue to keep contact, but both live in another state with their husbands."

"What is it that made you want to make an appointment to come in and see a psychiatrist?"

"I am getting to that. It took me a while to get myself here, so I thought it best for me to spell things out carefully for you. I'll get quickly to the point, and then I will elaborate. I think I killed a man, Dr. Tucci."

She waited to see his reaction, which was calm and attentive, so she felt that she could go on with her story. She picked up one of the glasses on the table, pointed to the small pitcher, and said, "May I, please.?"

Tucci poured some water and said, "Wet your whistle, and tell me more."

She relaxed when she knew he was not rattled by her comment.

"My husband, John, was thirteen years older than me. When he died after a major heart attack, I was left with a substantial amount of money. I had been a housewife most of my married life. I had never taken up a different career. John preferred it that way. After his death, I began to look for hobbies that I could get caught up in. I had always liked birds and going on jaunts with other birders offered pleasant companionship as well as learning about something I liked. There were times, though, when I would prefer to be alone and would sometimes explore areas on my own.

I had heard about a newly opened river area in a nearby county. I had been wanting to take pictures of water birds, so I packed up my binoculars and camera and planned a trip. I thought the territory was new to me, but when I got there, it had an eerie sense of familiarity, like a very old memory. Not being superstitious, I dismissed the feeling and proceeded to wander the riverbank taking pictures. At a bend in the river, I happened to look down to see two salamanders in what seemed to be a territorial struggle. When I looked up again, my eyes fixated on a very large cottonwood tree. I was startled. I shivered, and I saw in my mind what seemed to be a familiar face of a very handsome man. I did not know him, but somehow, I knew him. The salamanders, startled by my treading near them, scurried off, distracting me. When I looked up again, the man's face was gone, and the site had once again taken on a normal tone. I was left with an uneasy feeling, so much that I felt the need to high-tail it out of there, and I did. That evening at home, I couldn't seem to shake a feeling of dread. I woke up several times during the night with feelings of unease."

She stopped talking for a moment and shivered. "See, I have goosebumps now just talking about how I felt. I knew it was not real, but it felt real."

Dr. Tucci took the opportunity to ask a question. "Did this feeling and vivid sense of memory remind you of anything you had read or a story you had been told, or any other event you had experienced?"

"No, but the very next night I had a vivid dream of walking along that same river. There were some large cottonwood trees along the bank and a few seedlings. Somehow, I was now an attractive young woman who was struggling with strong feelings about a man. In the dream, I was sensing danger. I wanted to get away from there, but I felt compelled to continue my walk. As I approached the river, I looked over the bank and was startled to see the body of a young man lying partly in the water. I immediately woke from the dream, sweating and shaking profusely. I got up and made some coffee, and because I knew I did not want to attempt to sleep again for a while, I put a bit of rum in the coffee to settle my nerves. As I sat up drinking rum-laced coffee, I had the feeling that the woman in the dream was me, but she was beautiful, and I was always rather plain-looking. The dream seemed to be in an earlier time. I usually like to take my camera on nature walks, but in the dream, I carried a sketch pad and some charcoal. I was wearing a skirt, which I have not done in years. I wondered if I was re-experiencing an earlier life in the dream. Then I began to wonder if I might be having a nervous breakdown. It was then that I decided to see a psychiatrist, and the relief I felt about deciding to get help from a professional relaxed me enough to settle down and try to get some sleep – or maybe it was that second shot of rum. I called your office the next morning at the suggestion of a friend. I felt I would either get cured of madness or find out more about a previous life's impact on this one. Over the next couple of weeks, while I waited for the appointment, these thoughts about a previous life continued, and I continued to dream, strangely, often about salamanders fighting over territory, and I couldn't shake the feeling that I had somehow been responsible for someone's death."

Dr. Tucci felt the need to understand more about her life before delving into her fantasies. To better integrate how these emotional entanglements began, he would need to have more pieces of the puzzle.

"I'll tell you what - I need to have more building blocks about how you got to who you are in this life to be able to understand anything about any previous life. let's start by you telling me about some part of this life that gives you a good feeling or comfort. If I have questions, I will ask you. If you are comfortable with answering, go ahead. If not, we can put that topic off for another time when you might be ready."

"Thank you, Doctor. That sounds like a good way to start."

Beulah sat back in the chair and began to talk about her children.

"My two girls were the light of my life. I never loved anyone like I loved them – not even my parents. They were like a part of me. My parents were always there for me, but my girls were my joy! Even when they hit their teens and were testing out their independence, I would marvel at how they ultimately followed their common sense to make positive and level-headed choices most of the time. My husband was a good man but was raised by parents who grew up during the depression with rough times. He had a hard time shaking his family's fiscal rigidity and hard knocks mentality."

Beulah went on to talk about the thrill of watching her girls excel in school, become popular among their peers, and keep their heads on straight when it came to boys. She could not help but contrast her own upbringing to that of her girls. When her husband became too protective, she would ease him down. She did not want her girls to be enveloped in a protective sheath as she had been, knowing that it would become stifling. Her demeanor had changed when she spoke about her girls, as if it opened the windows to let fresh air into her own rather drab life. They carried on for another half hour with Dr. Tucci doing more listening than talking or asking questions. When the time was up, the issue about whether to continue was again approached.

"Dr. Tucci, do you think I am crazy?"

"I must admit I really don't know enough yet to put all the pieces of the puzzle together. I would like to know how it came to you that your experience might have come from another life and more about what you remember about that, as well as other experiences."

Beulah pondered for a moment. "I must admit that the idea of delving into this makes me feel anxious. I would like to think about it for a couple of days and get back to you, if I may."

Tucci smiled. "I think that's a good idea. Call me when you're ready, and I'll find a spot for you. It was good to meet you, and I hope you will allow me to continue to be helpful to you."

Beulah had never learned to trust people very much, but she felt relatively at ease with this man. He was not pushing her to continue, but he was offering help in a gentle way. Yet, somehow, she wanted to take a little time to consider whether she wanted to get into all the feelings that she sensed would be coming.

Chapter Two: The Police

Over the next two nights, Beulah had restless sleep. Her dreams, when she did doze off, were agitated. In one of these dreams, she had a brief but vivid image of taking a large hat-pin out of an older style hat that she was wearing and lunging forward with it, like using a rapier. When she awoke the next morning, she decided to go to the police and see what she could find out about any such assaults or worse.

Entering the station, the reception room had a large desk, several doors going to other areas, an elevator, and stairs going up to other rooms.

She approached the heavy-set officer at the desk and asked to see the person in charge.

"That would be me, ma'am."

"I'm here to inquire about any recent crimes where anyone was assaulted or otherwise injured."

"Were you aware of anyone reporting such a thing, ma'am?"

"No, sir. That's why I am here – to see if anyone has been hurt or assaulted. I am of the belief that I may be associated with something of that nature, and I want to check to be sure."

The policeman looked at her quizzically. He took down her name and contact information and listened as she described her intuition and dreams, including the description of the long hair pin. When she was finished, he said, "Ma'am, there have been no crimes in this county of the kind that you have described. If you continue to be troubled by these kinds of unsettling dreams, I strongly suggest that you see your doctor to get them checked out. If anything comes up, I have your contact information and will be able to get back in touch with you."

With that, Beulah thanked the policeman, who gave her a sympathetic smile, and then left the station.

"He thinks I'm nuts. That's for sure.", she said to herself. The decision was made. "Maybe I am nuts. I guess it's back to Dr. Tooch." She had liked the fact that the doc had shared his nickname with her.

Beulah returned home and called Dr. Tucci. He was able to get her back in the schedule within a week. He was as good as his word.

Within another hour, she received another phone call.

"Ms. Blanche? This is Sgt. Barnes at the police station. We spoke earlier today. I did some investigating after you left, and I would like to speak with you again. Can you come back down to the police station so we can continue with where we left off?"

"I would be happy to come back. Do you want me to schedule a time with you?"

"I would like you to come as soon as you can. Some important information has come up."

"I will try to be there within the hour. Thank you for calling back."

Beulah mused as she fed her cat, changed the litterbox, put out fresh drinking water, and looked around to see if there was anything else to do. With some trepidation, she put her coat back on and headed to her car. Once again, she drove to the police station, this time with more unease.

When she arrived, Sgt. Barnes eagerly approached her and asked her to join him in a private office with another man who was not in uniform.

"Ms. Blanche, this is detective Kraft. He is with the state police. He has some information about a situation in another county with some similarity to what you described to me earlier. He would like to hear more details about the experiences that you told me about."

"Hello, Ms. Blanche, nice to meet you. My name is John Kraft. Sgt. Barnes, here, tells me that you reported some interesting information to him that might help me to put some pieces of a puzzle together. Would you be willing to go over some details again with me?"

Beulah looked at him and knew something was amiss. Unlike Sgt. Barnes, who was tall and rather rotund, Detective Kraft was about five foot eight with a crew cut and a pencil-thin mustache. She estimated that he had bought his suit at Sears. She thought, "They got the big guns involved in a rather rapid fashion on whatever case this was." Whatever information her intuition or past life experiences had prodded her to come forward had rattled their cages. She began to get a premonition that this whole experience might complicate her life more than she had anticipated. She knew that Sgt. Barnes had already told detective Kraft about the details of her story, but she also knew that he wanted to see if she knew more, and if she was involved in some direct way.

"Of course, Detective Kraft. I am always ready to help the police with what I know or don't know."

The detective looked at her with gentleness. "Do you mind if I call you by your first name, Beulah?"

She smiled and said, "You may, detective. I am quite used to it."

They both knew that he was gingerly trying to soften her up.

"There were several things, Beulah, that Sgt. Barnes mentioned which could be quite helpful to me. Would you tell me about the body of the man that you saw in the river?"

"Well, I did not actually see a body in the river. I dreamt that I saw a body in the river, and it startled me so much that I immediately woke up, and I did not want to go back to sleep."

"Can you describe the body?"

"Well, yes, I'll do my best. He was, as best I can remember, a young man, I would guess in his early thirties, lying in the river face down, his head toward the bank. He had on dress pants and a nice shirt, but no jacket. His hair was a reddish-brown color."

"Beulah, what was it about the large hair pin that you told Sgt. Barnes? Was it part of the dream, or something else?"

"Oh, no. That was a totally different dream. In that dream, I was being accosted by someone and was using the hat pin to defend myself. The strange thing is that I don't have a hat like that, nor a long hat pin. Truth is, I wouldn't be caught dead wearing a hat like that. However, in all of those strange dreams I have been having since these weird feelings and apparitions have begun, I am wearing older style clothes, like those worn around the turn of the twentieth century."

"Have you told anyone else besides me and Sgt. Barnes about these experiences?"

"Only Dr. Tucci, my psychiatrist. I saw him for the first time a few days ago and plan to see him again in about a week. With all that I was experiencing, I thought it best to get some professional help."

"Would that be Dr. John Tucci?"

"Yes, it is."

"We have had the pleasure of working with Dr. Tucci in the past as a consultant on some other cases. Would you allow us to speak with him about you?"

"I will have to discuss that with him before I give you permission, but I would like to help in any way that I can."

"Thank you, Beulah. I will probably want to speak with you again as we proceed with our investigation. Incidentally, do you happen to know anyone in Pierce County or have any relatives there?"

"No, I don't know anyone there personally, but that is where I did go birding when this whole weird experience started. And I keep thinking about those fighting salamanders from that visit there."

"Salamanders?" Detective Kraft looked quizzically at Beulah.

"Well, Beulah, let's wind it up for today. We'll be back in touch. Thank you for coming in to talk to us today."

As she left, Beulah thought, "Dr. Tooch, here I come."

Chapter Three:
Putting Pieces Together

After Beulah left the station, Detective Kraft and Sgt. Barnes put their heads together. The Sergeant spoke first.

"See what I meant? She seems to know some details that she doesn't seem to be aware of in other ways. She talked as though she was unfamiliar with the area where the body was found. She's either a good actress or she's channeling something beyond my ability to understand."

Kraft looked puzzled. "But her description of the kind of weapon, the way the body was found in the river, the location of the field and the cottonwoods, and even the numerous salamanders in that area. And this whole thing about the psychiatrist. Is she building a case for insanity in case she's involved? And she picks Tucci. She might have known that we use him as a consultant."

Barnes was equally puzzled. "A hat pin from an outdated hat? Who would have thought of that? The bloody ice pick we found would not have pointed us to a woman assailant. And she came to us. Why do that?"

There was not enough to go on yet, but Beulah was certainly a person of interest. They decided to have another plain clothes detective follow and track her movements, phone calls, and investigate her contacts, social and otherwise. They would need to know more about her background, her social life, her family, essentially everything. Yet, somehow, this pleasant little old lady had a presence about her that threw them off. The pieces didn't fit. Why would she come to them to tell them about a murder that she may have been involved with? She didn't seem to even know who was killed or why. She had an awareness of some of the details, but not exactly spot on. Maybe she was just a crazy person, but she presented enough information that they had to find out more.

They were secretly glad that she was seeing Tucci. They knew that he could not give them information that she related to him in confidence unless she gave him permission, but they tended to trust Tucci to work with them as much as he could. They also knew that he had a knack for working with people who had weird ways of thinking about things. If anyone could get into this lady's head, it would be "The Tooch".

There were still a lot of unanswered questions in this case. They still had not properly identified the victim. There were no defensive wounds on his body. He had three deep stab wounds to the chest which fit the bloody ice pick found on the river-bank. There were no prints on the weapon, so the killer must have been wearing gloves. The victim was well dressed in a suit and tie, which really did not fit the area by the river where he was found. The first thing that they had to do was to find out who this well-dressed handsome young man was and what he was doing in that attire in a rather isolated field by the river.

CHAPTER FOUR: INTO THE PUDDLE

Within a week, Dr. Tucci was able to get Beulah scheduled again. They spent the first fifteen minutes or so going back over her experience with the police. When Tucci asked her if any of her conversation with them had triggered any new feelings or experiences, she reiterated that it just brought back the memories that she had talked about with him. He then began to ask her more questions about her marriage. A rather bland countenance swept over her as she began to talk about her husband. To her surprise, after listening to her drone on about that relationship, Dr. Tucci dozed off.

She was incensed. "Dr. Tucci!! Don't you dare fall asleep while I am talking to you!"

Tucci opened his eyes and said, "I just had a dream about you. You were younger and carried yourself in a rather attractive manner, but you were tearful and angry. It was as if someone had somehow hurt you, either physically or emotionally. It was hard to tell. And you said, 'I didn't mean to. I'm sorry, I'm really very sorry, but I was angry.'

Does any of that mean anything to you?"

Beulah looked startled, and there was a sudden pallor to her face.

"How did you know that? Who did you talk to about me? Have the police investigated my history or background? Even if they did, there is no one who would know anything that personal about me."

Tucci answered softly, "I spoke to no one about you, but it sounds like it's up to you to start talking about it with me, or you will be wasting time for us both."

Beulah stared at him without talking for several minutes.

Tucci continued to look at her and just waited. Tears began to well up in her eyes. Tucci continued to wait. She finally said, "I have had some painful times that I have managed to hold down for a long time. I thought they were under control."

Tucci again spoke softly, "We tend to keep them stuffed away and out of sight, but they do tend to leak out when we least expect it. When that happens, it's best to have someone there to help sort it out, or it tends to fester. Ready to tell me about it?"

She continued to be hesitant, but he could tell that she had surrendered to his soft appeal and was wanting to begin healing those old wounds.

She said, "I don't know where to start."

Tucci replied, "You've already told me some of the comfortable parts about your children. Maybe it's time to start to uncover some of the pain. Perhaps we should start with this person?"

Beulah continued to ponder. She wondered how this information had popped up out of nowhere. Was this guy psychic? It was too accurate to be a lucky guess. He did seem to fall into a sleep. The whole experience awakened in her a desire to know more about what this person could do to help her be more alive. She was already excited by the experience. Her curiosity was aroused. She decided to dig in.

"Let me start by telling you about Eddie. I both loved and hated him. Eddie was a long time ago, but an era in my life that still hangs with me."

She started her story of love and hate. She was sixteen and enjoying school. She had a lot of friends in her younger grades, but as she got into high school, she realized that a lot of her friends began to take an interest in boys and wanted to spend more time flirting with them, so she also began to take an interest in fitting in. She had no siblings and had few other models to imitate. Her parents were loving but stern, so they, as models, were not of a playful nature. In short, her social skills and ability to fit in with her crowd were rather naïve and limited. Then she met Eddie. He was flamboyant and cocky, but popular. He was a year and a half older as well. She was intrigued by him and soon became infatuated. Looking back now, she could see that his primary interest in her was sexual, and he enjoyed his ability to have a strong emotional hold on her.

"He was a good-looking boy who was very athletic. He was co-captain of the football team and was also on the basketball team. He was older than me, so I was thrilled when I saw that he took an interest in me. I was both thrilled and surprised. I knew that I did not have the figure nor the cute face that automatically attracted boys, so I thought maybe it was the fact that I smiled a lot. I was quite naïve."

Tucci sat quietly and listened. He did not want to interrupt the flow of her thought. There was plenty of time to ask questions when the time came.

"Eddie was quite the charmer when he wanted to be. Later, I found him to be quite the jerk, especially when he didn't get what he wanted. He began to groom me. I found out what that word meant sometime later and realized then how he had done it. He took me to the movies several times, usually alone, and proceeded to kiss me, and gradually we got into heavier petting. Eventually he borrowed his parents' car, and we ended up in a secluded place. The kissing got hot and heavy. He began to touch my breasts. I wanted him to stop, but as I backed away, he started to get angry, and I did not want to upset him, so I let him continue. He looked at me and said, 'Don't worry, I've got a rubber.' Before I knew it, he had reached up under my dress and pulled my panties down and was kneeling above me. It was quick, and I realized that he had not bothered to use any protection. I was bewildered and stunned as I suddenly thought about the possibility of getting pregnant. He quickly pulled up his pants. I did the same. Then he said, 'I'd better get you home.' He drove me home. There was not much conversation until he dropped me at my front door. Then he said, 'I'll call you soon.'

I didn't hear from him until I saw him at school talking in his charming way to one of the cheerleaders. I heard him say to her, 'I'll pick you up at seven.' He looked over in my direction, saw me, winked at me, and walked in the other direction. I was crushed."

She stopped talking momentarily and wiped tears from both eyes.

"I tried to hang on to the excitement of having a boy who seemed to like me, but the hoped-for connection faded as Eddie continued his pursuit of the cheerleader. He was public about his flirtation with her, which he never was with me. I eventually realized that once he had gotten into my pants, it was just another notch on his gun, so to speak. I was gradually more aware of waking up to my anger at what he had done to me. I worried for about two weeks about possibly being pregnant but was relieved when I got my period. I grew to detest him, but I carried the excitement of his deception with me as well, my first real sexual experience, as clumsy and uncomfortable as it was. So, you can see, doc, it became both thrilling and heartbreaking, and I carried both the feelings of love and hate for him, and sometimes found it hard to separate them."

Dr. Tucci waited a moment and said to her, "What were you sorry about when you said that you didn't mean it and that you were very sorry?"

Beulah looked at him and said, "That was what you said when you fell asleep and said you had a dream about me."

Tucci said, "But the dream was about you, and you were quite reactive to those words. Did you have another encounter with this guy, Eddie, that resulted in something that you regretted even more?"

She looked puzzled. "There were times when I felt like I had had encounters with him that I do not really remember. I don't know if they were dreams that slipped out of my awareness after waking up or if they were daydreams of some kind."

Tucci waited for more to come. Then he asked, "Have you had the experience of finding yourself doing things and not remembering how you ended up being in this place at this time or what you have been up to for the last several hours?"

"Yes", she said. "Sometimes I feel I have been daydreaming and don't have a sense of what I have been up to for a while, as though I have been on automatic pilot while I have been taking care of things, but my head has been somewhere else."

"How long do these automatic pilots last?"

"It's funny. Sometimes a matter of several minutes, sometimes a matter of hours. I always assumed I was just bored with what I was doing, and my mind took a vacation."

"That is probably one of the better ways of describing it. Have you ever come back to the present with an eerie feeling or sense of dread or fear?"

"Occasionally I do have a sense of relief to come back to whatever mundane task I am doing rather than being in a day-dream."

"Has anyone ever told you that your sense of humor is different from time to time, depending on the people or circumstances around you?"

"These questions are getting a little weird, Dr. Tooch."

"I'm not asking them to make you uncomfortable, but to try to understand how your mind may be working to protect you from uncomfortable feelings by helping you to escape them. Perhaps I should give you a shot at me and ask if you have any questions for me that I may have stirred up in you?"

"Well, Doc, a lot of these questions are tending to push buttons in me that edge into my discomfort zone, and this whole process seems to be leaning me in that direction. However, at the same time, I have this sense of a kind of excitement that as I get into it more, I may have the opportunity to understand myself better and maybe climb myself out of this slump of boredom that I tend to find myself in. My question to you, is what are you getting out of this? Why do you do this kind of work? Isn't it a bit voyeuristic?"

"That's a very reasonable question. What do I get out of this kind of work? Well, first of all, it's interesting and keeps my brain working like figuring out a puzzle. Secondly, I really do think that it helps people to learn to live their lives happier. And then I find that I get to know people as they really are, rather than the front they put up for others. I see them as more real, and they often appreciate that in the long run."

"Do they all like you to know who they really are?"

"No, but often they will eventually come to appreciate coming to that realization about themselves and accept it for themselves, and that is the important part. It's more meaningful to them, when I don't get to take the credit and they figure it out for themselves."

Beulah was quiet for a few moments. She recognized that this guy made it easier to talk to him because he was very upfront with her, and he seemed to be kind and not just in it for himself.

Tucci waded through the silence for a few moments and then said, "Are you up for talking about Eddie a little more?"

"Yes, it took me too long to let go of my thrilling feelings for him. I should say it took me too long to see him for who he really was and to let my feelings for him change to what they should have been. I was a naïve kid, and he knew it and took advantage of that weakness in me. I clung to my distorted sense of excitement for him much too long, so that when the bubble finally burst, I lost it. I lost it to the point that I actually lost track of several days that I still have trouble remembering."

"Do you have snatches of memory from that time, or is it a total blank?"

"I have some dream-like pieces of memory, but they are difficult to piece together."

"What was Eddie like during that time of the bubble, before it burst?"

"He pretended occasionally to be sweet to me, but it was usually in private, when we happened to encounter each other alone. He even arranged to meet me in the park one evening. I was reluctant but somehow still hanging on to hope. We walked along one of the paths and found a rather secluded area where we talked for a while. It began to get dark. He said he missed me. We began to kiss, and he began to grope me. I told him that it was not a good time to be doing this. I was very uncomfortable and told him so. He started to get angry, but I said, 'it's getting dark. We'd better go.' We tidied up and quickly took the path back. Again, there were few words spoken until we got near my house, and he said again, 'I will give you a call.' I got home and felt degraded. I finally realized how furious I was. I wanted to kill him. For the next day or more, I don't remember much.

The following week I happened to be in the bathroom at school when I heard someone crying in one of the toilet stalls. I asked if she needed help. She stopped crying, came out of the stall, wiping tears. It was the cheerleader that I had overheard being asked out by Eddie. She broke into tears again. "I'm pregnant".

"Was it Eddie?"

"How did you know?".

"I worried about the same thing with him."

She cried again. I tried to comfort her. I suggested she tell her mother. It was the kind of thing that would need a supportive family. We became pretty good friends after that. Eddie became my worst enemy from that point on." Beulah was quiet again for a few minutes.

Tucci looked at her kindly. It had been an intense session. He knew that she would likely rebound. At the same time, he did not want to push her too hard, or she might feel some reluctance to returning. There was more to pursue, but was it in another life as she thought, or was it another aspect of this life and a way for her to defend herself against painful awareness?

"I think it's time we called it a day. Let's allow some of these notions to sink in and plan to meet weekly for a while. I am sure you will have more questions for me as I will have for you. Same time, same day next week work for you? "

Beulah took a deep breath of relief and eased out of her chair. "See you then, Dr. Tooch. Thank you."

"Remember, if you need to call me before our appointment, I will make myself available."

He watched her walk toward the door. She looked tired but resolved. He realized that he was also a bit drained but encouraged as well.

Chapter Five: More Digging

Detective Kraft continued his search for information about the murder. In the process he looked at other mysterious deaths that had taken place over the past years in the area. There were three others, and all were men. One was a blunt force trauma to the head, possibly accidental, one was a brutal beating, and the last was found to have been a poisoning, and it was unclear whether it was self-inflicted. They had no apparent connection, but they all occurred within fifty miles of each other, and all within the past three years. The other detective who had been instructed to track Beulah had, so far, not come up with much. He noted that she met with her birding group and that she still attended a hospice grief group on occasion.

Something about Beulah's information, while lacking details of the murder investigation, continued to plague Kraft. He had never believed in extrasensory phenomena, and there was just too much similarity in her dreams and perceptions and the facts of the case to be entirely coincidental. He wanted to dig into her marriage, her relationships, her life. He knew that this was the kind of information that a guy like Tucci could resurrect, but he also knew that Tucci would never give it up without permission, and permission would not be likely. Kraft would have to find it the hard way, by good old digging up dirt.

So far, they had come up empty. Beulah had never had any legal problems, not so much as a traffic ticket. He thought that he would start by looking at her friends and acquaintances and into any major changes in her life from her school years to her married years and to the time before and after her husband's death. It was about all he had to work with until he got something that might lead him elsewhere.

The police did identify the most recent victim. He was a businessman who had owned a jewelry store in a small town. He was single and in his mid-thirties. His police record was clean. He was not known to be a gambler. His business was doing reasonably well. No one seemed to have a clue about why he was found dead in such an area, dressed like he would be in his business and not for a remote trip to the river. The investigative team was looking into his family contacts, his business practices, and his medical records for any other pertinent information that might help to give them a clue about why someone would want to kill him, and why he might have been where he was found. They had a lot of ground to cover yet. Kraft knew that he had to keep digging until he found some answers. Among his next steps, as he saw it, was to start looking into Beulah's now-deceased husband. Since she was still on his list of people of interest, Kraft wanted to know more about her personal interactions.

"Get out the shovel.", Kraft said to himself.

Chapter Six: Soft Persistence

Dr. Tucci was glad that Beulah arrived at her next appointment without giving any hint of reluctance. She smiled and nodded towards the chair where she had sat the last time, as though it was a query about whether she should make herself comfortable there again. Tucci nodded and pointed to the water pitcher and glass with a tilt of his head to ask if she wanted some. "Yes, please.", was her reply. Tucci knew that they had hit on a lot of potentially touchy matters in her last session, and he did not want to push her too hard, but he did want to pursue enough information to understand her lapses of memory, and how they impacted her life. He decided to start by giving her a chance to begin the session with any impressions or concerns she might have had after the session a week ago.

"Hello, Beulah. Nice to see you again. How did your week go?"

"I spent the week thinking a lot about the lapses in my recollection about things. I had not paid that much attention to them before, but our conversation last week provoked a lot of thought. I would like to know more about what that is all about."

Tucci was glad that she seemed to have more curiosity than fear. He felt that would allow them to proceed more smoothly to explore her psychic defenses and hopefully, to accept them in a helpful way.

"So, what have your thoughts been about these lapses? I think your thoughts about them might as useful as mine." Indeed, he himself believed this.

Beulah smiled. She was grateful that he was willing to accept her musings on the matter. "I remember your talking about looking at how my mind might use 'defenses' to protect me from my own feelings. I thought that was an intriguing idea, and possibly quite true. I have been through a lot of times that, looking back, felt quite nasty."

"Have you given more thought this past week about some of those nasty parts of your life? Are there some that you might want to start out with today? We can take them as they come and as you feel ready to bring them up."

She paused. It was as if she were still wondering about how much she really wanted to dig in.

Tucci took the opportunity to ask, "By the way, whatever happened to that guy Eddie? How did he end up after everyone finished high school? Did he pursue college? A football career? Selling cars? Did anyone ever find out that he raped you?"

Beulah looked at him and said, "That's about as good a place to start with the nastier parts of my life as any. Eddie dug his own hole and didn't stop digging until he buried himself. Emma, the cheerleader that he had impregnated, ended up getting a back-alley abortion and nearly dying. She didn't want to tell her parents, so she went to Eddie who arranged it. He didn't know what he was doing, and it was a mess. She ended up in the hospital in intensive care. Her story came out, and the truth came out. Eddie was lucky he was not arrested. Emma's parents did not want to put her through any more suffering, so they did not press charges, but he was kicked off the football team and eventually other athletics. He dropped out of school and never graduated." She smiled while she told this story to Tucci.

"I can see from your expression that you took some pleasure in Eddie's downfall."

"I hate to admit it, because I got to really like Emma, and I was glad that his behavior caught up with him for what he did to her. He eventually was killed about ten years after high school in some kind of altercation behind a bar. I think he was stabbed or beaten to death."

"How old were you when you started having lapses in your memory or daydreams that took you away for periods of time?

Was that before or after your encounters with Eddie?"

"As a younger child, I did have daydreams that took me away, but I must admit, I did have them more after that first sexual encounter. After the rape, I began to be more intent in finding other girls that he had dated and then dropped. I got to know some of them well. Some of them became good friends and we would sometimes get together to talk. We often talked about Eddie and his 'romantic forays'. As I look back, I think I began to have more of those escaping 'daydreams' at that time in my life. I think I am beginning to see now how I might have been using them to help me defend myself against feelings, as you mentioned the last time we met. Thank you for steering my thoughts in that direction."

Tucci gave her a whisper of a smile. He said, "I guess that's my job, to help you to come to think things through for yourself. Do you have friends who recount things that you have said or done that you don't recall, but that they found funny or strange or maybe out of character for you?"

"Yes, I often find them strange or funny myself when I hear what I said or did. I say to myself, I really said that or did that? Then we all laugh at it."

Tucci looked at her and said, "Any that stand out or come to mind?"

She blushed a bit and told him that one time they were together and telling stories. She mentioned that she had heard a funny limerick, but couldn't remember where or when, but it had stuck in her head.

She said that it went like this,

"There once was a man from Madras,

Whose balls were made out of brass,

When in stormy weather,

They clanged loudly together,

And Lightning shot out of his ass."

She grinned as she told Tucci that once they heard it, they howled, and afterward they would always refer to Eddie as the man from Madras. "When they first started saying this about him, they had to remind me about the limerick that I had told. I had forgotten all about it."

Tucci smiled but waited a little longer to reply. "It almost sounds like you might have been sleepwalking in a kind of way during some of those times with friends."

Beulah pondered what he said. "Being with those girls was like an escape for me from other parts of my life. I did enjoy being with them, but I did do a lot of daydreaming when I was with them."

Tucci softly, but quickly pounced. "From what other parts of your life were you needing to escape?"

Her brow furrowed. "My parents, I guess, but mainly myself. I had learned not to like myself, and my parents didn't help much with that. There was this feeling that I must have been a different person at one time. Maybe that is where the feeling that I had had a previous better life had originated, but it was almost too strong a feeling not to be true."

Tucci looked at her gently. "Part of my job is to help you to sort out what is feeling and what is fact. We need to look at different facets of that. When you are ready, it would likely be helpful if you could tell me more about your parents and your relationship with them over time, and what impact it had on you. Meanwhile, I am wondering if there might be another part of you, something hidden, that you might sense, but that continues to yet remain quiet to you. Have you ever wondered what part of you takes over when you are daydreaming, perhaps as if you were sleepwalking?"

"I need to ponder that one. I know that our time is almost up. I think I need to take some time and think about all we spoke about today. Will we be meeting at the same time and day next week?"

"Same day, same time. Have a good week. Any problems,

don't hesitate to call me."

Chapter Seven: Being Shadowed

On her way home, Beulah decided to check out one of her old high school pals. Lisa Barnes worked in a pet store at a nearby mall and didn't really need to work. She had been married to a relatively wealthy man but was also widowed. Since she loved animals and liked to interact with people, she kept her old job. She had been one of the gang of gals who had encountered Eddie back in high school. She and Beulah had continued to be friends and tended to keep in touch about once a month. Beulah wanted to share her new shrink adventure with her old friend.

She parked her car near the pet store. As she unbuckled her seat belt, she glanced in the rear-view mirror. Oddly she saw a car she had noted earlier that day. She wouldn't have paid that much attention to it except that she had noticed the license plate. It was 007 NSS. She had chuckled at it earlier when she thought of James Bond as 007 and the initials as being the first letters for No Shit Sherlock. It was a bit peculiar that she would have seen it in two quite different parts of town. As she got out of her car, she noted that the gentleman stayed in his and was writing something on a notepad. It had definitely roused her curiosity. After locking the car, she went into the pet store to see Lisa, hoping to take her out for coffee. As luck would have it, Lisa was there and ready to step out for a break. Remembering the car with the funny license plate, Beulah asked Lisa if they could sneak out the back way today. Lisa cocked her head to the side in that inimitable questioning way that all the girls in the old gang knew.

"Babe, are you up to your old tricks again?" Most of the old gang had got to calling her Babe. It was a lot chummier than Beulah. It had started from BB for Beulah Blanche and moved to BeeBee and naturally curled into just plain old Babe as they got more familiar.

"Whatever do you mean, Lisa?" She answered with a generous smile.

Lisa was always up for a good prank, so they snuck out the back way and took a circuitous route to the coffee shop. They sat in a booth, and Lisa eagerly wanted to hear what the drama was all about.

"OK, Babe, have you got a new man in your life, or have you won the lottery?"

"Well, now that you mention it, I do have a new man in my life, but not in the way you're thinking. In fact, I suddenly have several new men in my life." She went on to tell Lisa about her birding experience, her visits to Dr. Tucci, her questioning by detective Kraft, and the interesting car with the funny license plate.

"Wow, you suddenly do have a lot going on. Are you in any kind of trouble? Anything I can do to help?"

"I really don't know what the hell Is going on. I'm trying to figure out if I'm crazy, if my brain is pulling tricks on me, or if I've been walking around in a dream for the last month or more. That license plate puts the frosting on the cake, unless the police have someone following me. I guess that would make the most sense. If that guy is still parked there when we get back, that would be my best guess. Yes, that probably would make the most sense. But, why? We did some mean things, but we didn't kill anyone."

"Are you forgetting about what happened to Eddie?"

"I remember reading about it in the paper."

"Well, maybe your mind is playing tricks on you, with all these weird dreams you have been having lately. Are you having one of those 'absentee spells' that you used to have when you got stressed?"

There was another pause.

Lisa broke the tension with, "Hey, we're supposed to be catching up. How are those kids of yours doing?"

For the next half hour, they tracked their families together. It was time for Lisa to get back to the shop, and they took the same route back, again using the back door. They hugged, and Beulah left by the front door. She looked at the spot where the other car had been. It was gone, but as she was about to enter hers, she saw it parked in a different spot. The driver again pulled out his pad and wrote something. When she pulled out of the lot, she saw his car start up and begin to leave.

"So that's it," she said to herself, "the cops have put a tail on me."

She drove home. When she got there, she tried to focus on various mundane chores around the house and in her yard, but she continued to attempt to sort out the events of her day – with Tucci, with Lisa, and the car with the weird license plate. When she found herself putting things away in places other than where she habitually placed them, she knew she was seriously distracted. She knew that these thoughts would be swimming through her head for the next week until her next appointment with Tucci. She finally picked up the phone and called him. No answer, so she left a message on his answering machine. She knew she would have to call again in the morning. She poured herself a cup of steaming water from the hot water tap that she had had installed and started looking for a tea bag when the phone rang. It was Tucci.

"I got your message. How can I help?"

"You said that I could call if I needed anything before our appointment. I do think I need to meet sooner than our scheduled time. My brain feels in a twirl."

"Is it feeling urgent?"

"I think, sort of, at least to me."

"I could get to you this evening around 7:30, or tomorrow morning some time. What works better for you?"

"I don't want to take up your private evening time."

"What works better for you?"

"This evening at 7:30 is best."

"I'll be happy to meet you this evening at the office. Don't be concerned. I didn't have any plans. I'll see you then."

Suddenly feeling relieved, she smiled and thought laughingly, "I hope I'm not getting addicted to this guy". The teabag went into her cup and swished around. After removing the bag, a splash of rum was added for good measure, and she sipped at it. Contemplating the day, her thoughts meandered back through high school days and time with Eddie and with the friends accrued back then. Her conversation with Lisa vividly jarred the fact that she did have a lot of holes in her memory. Maybe her brain was busy in its own way with protecting her from unpleasantries. She'd like to explore that further with Dr. T.

Chapter Eight: Beginning of Phantasy's Ending

Beulah was both nervous and excited as she entered the building where Dr. T. had his office. It seemed strange to again be visiting a doctor after hours, but she was grateful that he was so accommodating. When she entered his office suite and saw his welcoming smile, she surprised herself by breaking into tears, something she had not done for years. She blushed at the same time with embarrassment. She suddenly thought of the phrase from Yeats' poem, 'The Second Coming',

"Things fall apart; the centre cannot hold;

Mere anarchy is loosed upon the world,

The blood-dimmed tide is loosed and everywhere

The ceremony of innocence is drowned;"

Tucci looked at her and said, "Beulah, I think you should take a seat and give yourself a moment or two to collect your thoughts. Then we'll have a chance to start from wherever you feel is a good launching place."

Beulah thought to herself, "Sure he will have me start, and he'll divert the conversation to where he wants it to go, but that's OK. He seems to direct me eventually to think about stuff that I would never have gotten to on my own." She wiped the tears away with a handkerchief as she said, "Sorry."

Tucci gave her a benevolent smile and said, "This place has been inundated with tears over the years. It's part of the décor. If they didn't evaporate as quickly as they were produced, this office would be underwater. No need for apologies. Besides, we need to irrigate the water lilies." He pointed to the Monet across the room.

After a brief gathering of herself, Beulah started. "After I left your office today, I met with an old friend." She told him about their reminiscing about old times, about noticing the car and the man who seemed to be tracking her movements, about avoiding him by using the back door, but finding him still waiting for her in the parking lot. "The thing that is troubling me the most is the fact that I am more and more aware that over the years, I have had chunks of time that I do not remember. My friends are aware of it in me but accept that as part of me. I've deduced that during those times I may seem like a different person and may even be more fun to be with. Yet there are swaths of time that they talk about with me that I don't recall, and I need to piece together with you what has been happening."

"When we first met, you spoke of a dream-like state where you felt like you were a different person at a different time. Have you had other incidents or dreams like that?"

"Sometimes in my dreams."

"In your sleep dreams or your awake dreams?"

"Both, I guess."

"Does it ever feel like maybe you are two people living in the same house, so to speak?"

"You mean like in the same body?" There was a long pause, and with a quizzical look, she said, "Maybe. I hadn't put it that way to myself until you asked."

"Would you mind if we tried something together? I would like to see if we could get you to relax enough, after a very stressful day, to find out if you have a companion part of you that is helping you to cope with difficulties. I would like to see if that other part of you would like to come out and talk to me. Would that be okay with you?"

"If you can help me to relax, I am up for whatever you want to try, Dr. T."

She was sitting in a comfortable chair. Tucci's office was more like a living room with his desk over by a window against the wall. He also had what looked like a living room chair, but a bit firmer and more straight-backed, facing the one in which Beulah sat.

Tucci took over speaking softly, almost in a monotone. "I want you to put your head back in the chair and take some deep breaths." After a few moments, he asked her to imagine she was lying on a grassy slope looking up at cumulus clouds and marveling at the shapes, some like faces, some like animals, some like angels with wings, but all living in the same clouds, making the clouds look like a repository of beautiful things, but also of some angry and rumbling troublesome things. Yet the clouds had it all under control. He asked if she thought any of these parts of the cloud could separate from the main cloud on an adventure of its own, and if so, could talk to him. He watched as a hint of a smile formed on her face.

"Will you come out and talk to me for a while, friend of Beulah? I am also here to help her, as you know."

Beulah responded in a soft and pleasant voice. "I thought you would never ask. Thank you for helping us." She opened her eyes with a twinkle, much like when she had spoken about her daughters.

Tucci asked gently, "Can we start by telling me the name you would like to be called?"

"I like to go by Ruth. Like the old biblical story, Ruth was the one who said, 'whither thou goest, I will go' and whither Beulah goes, I tag along. Makes it easier to keep her out of trouble."

"She hasn't really been aware of you, has she?"

"No, she has some vague memories, but she somehow thinks they occurred in a different time or a different world. I have kept her in the dark, mainly to keep her safe and unaware of some of the unsavory events that have happened over the years. She would tend to focus on them and drive herself mad. Not good for either of us."

"I would venture a guess that some of those episodes would have something to do with Eddie."

"Well, Doc, you are tuned into the right station."

"How long have you been in the picture and helping her out?"

"I've been around since she was a little girl. I helped her learn to lie to her parents – rather, I learned to lie for her. They were strict and tended to be punitive, so I helped us escape some paddling. I didn't come out a lot in those early years, but when adolescence arrived, I felt the need more often."

"After Eddie, were there other men that Beulah had strong feelings for, either positive or negative?"

"There were several, but mainly because of the pain that they had caused for the group of friends that had accumulated during Eddie's varied conquests, as well as the other horny high school boys who preyed on younger girls."

"Sounds like that group of friends rallied around each other."

"I thought of us as 'The Merry Mags', short for the Mary Magdalen Vigilantes – women who had seen the underside of some of the men around us, but who were 'finding another way to deal with them."

"Did being vigilantes include finding ways to get even? Being vigilantes usually infers taking some action to solve the problems."

"Yes, sometimes we managed to get even."

"Whatever really happened to Eddie?"

"He died."

"Do you know more about the details of his death?"

"None that I want to talk about right now."

"OK, maybe another time when you feel we are both ready. Did Beulah ever find any boys that she trusted or felt good about?"

"There was a guy named Clark that she developed a sort

of friendship with. He was from a poor family and had an after-school job, so he didn't hang around the school much for activities, but he seemed to be kind and respectful to her, and she seemed to like him, but never really let herself get overly attached to him."

"What was it about her husband that drew her to him?"

"Ah, you're a crafty one, Doc. You got me out here just to find out more about Beulah, didn't you?"

"Well, isn't that the whole idea of this process? I need to get to know her well enough to help her. And to help you and any others who might be hiding around the corner, ready to help her in a pinch. Speaking of which, are there any others? I'm sure as the chief helper, you would know them."

"You know what Doc? I think I have a new nickname for you. I'm going to call you 'The Unraveler'. I think I see where you are going with all this."

"But to unravel something allows us to work together to put it back together in a way that helps it work better, don't you think? Isn't that what Beulah really wanted when she first sought my help? And wasn't that what you really wanted as well? I would surmise that you were very influential in getting her to pick up the phone to call me in the first place. If so, then let's get to work."

"I'm not sure that Beulah is quite ready yet, Doc. I can feel her squirming to get out."

"Then let's ease up for today. I'll speak with Beulah again for a while, but when I need to speak to you again, I'll ask to speak to you as Ruth."

Ruth dropped her chin slightly onto her chest and seemed to doze briefly, then raised her head to look into Tucci's eyes.

"It felt like I dozed a bit. Sorry. That wasn't very polite."

"Was it one of those daytime dreams that you talked about?"

"Must have been."

"Any recollection of what the dream was about?"

"It was a bit of a jumble. It seemed we were talking about my parents and maybe about high school experiences or things along that line."

"Perhaps we have had enough for today. I think the relaxation you reached today will help. We can continue to work on unraveling and mending when we get together again. We'll try to keep it at your pace, but I want to reassure you that we seem to be making progress. I suspect that some of what we talked about will begin to come back to you in the meanwhile and will be reassuring."

They then arranged another visit in two days.

Chapter Nine: The Shovel is Out

Detective Kraft sat at his desk staring at the piles of notes, bits of newspaper articles, copies of old police reports, and his half-filled cup of cold coffee. He had continued to pursue his case, but also began to look into other homicides or "accidental" deaths over the years in the same geographical area to see if there were any similarities. He found a couple more in addition to the three that had happened within recent years. These additional deaths included a stabbing victim and another young man who died with a fractured skull. Both had been quite a few years ago, but coincidentally, both had lived in the same rough vicinity as the others, and the earlier two had attended the same high school, though not in the same class. Kraft had a sense that all of them might be connected somehow, including the fresh murder on his agenda. It was a bit of a guess, but it might be worth looking into people who had worked in the schools in the area and who might have known some of the deceased.

In addition to speaking with the recent victim's family, his associates, and people who knew him from his jewelry business, detective Kraft also shifted his attention to some of the older cases. He managed to make some connections with some of the older retired teachers from the high school to talk to them about "teaching in the old days", which he managed by getting invited to talk about "modern police work" at a care facility for older retired individuals. They were more than eager to talk about the variety of students that they had managed, and they fed Kraft a lot of helpful information about the youth culture and shenanigans at the time. Then, occasionally he would stop by to have coffee with some of them to pick up further bits of information.

Over time, Kraft was gleaning the fields, using a rake more than a shovel. As he scoured over the reports of the various victims and his notes from various interviews, he was aware that some of them had been accused of assaults of their own. Apparently, none had gone to trial or been charged with even a misdemeanor. Several had been athletes in high school. All this information just hung there like tennis shoes over a power line. Kraft knew it was a thing that kids did, but he could never really put any sense into it. Beulah's puzzle was also baffling. There were a lot of pieces, but he was not sure there was just one puzzle. One piece that was missing was why this independent jewelry store owner was wandering about in a rural field near a river dressed like he would at work in a small downtown store? Kraft couldn't help but wonder if a woman was involved in some way, like maybe an affair. Or perhaps with another man. All in all, lots yet to explore.

Chapter 10: The Net Expands

Shortly before her next visit with Dr. Tucci, Beulah answered her phone. It was Lisa Barnes. Lisa was rattled.

"Hey, Babe, remember when we went out for coffee last week, and you were concerned about someone might be following you? Well, now someone seems to be following me. What in the world did you tell those cops that you went to see? Are they on to some of our old stuff?"

"What old stuff are you talking about?"

"You know. Eddie, and then that other guy problem the Mary Mags took care of."

"I didn't tell the cops anything about any old stuff. I just told them about my recent weirdness and dreams and that I was checking to see if there was anything reported about what I was dreaming about. I told them I was seeing a shrink to see if I was going off my rocker. They thought I was this batty old lady and sent me home, but then called me back to get more information. They never asked me about anything that happened way back then."

"Well, that's good, but whatever is going on, they seem to be keeping an eye on me since your visit. Better be careful what you tell that shrink of yours as well. I don't want to get in any trouble after all these years."

After Lisa hung up, Beulah felt a bit perplexed. She mused to herself, "What about Eddie? He's been long gone. I didn't talk to anyone but Dr. Tooch about him."

She got her purse together, put her coat on and headed out the door to her appointment.

When she arrived, she was obviously a bit perplexed. Dr. Tucci noted her preoccupation, pointed to the chair, poured her a glass of water, and waited.

Beulah sat for a few moments contemplating, then put her head back against the chair, closed her eyes, and relaxed. She opened her eyes, smiled, and said, "OK, Dr. Tooch, it's Ruth. Let's get to work."

Tucci proffered an accepting smile. "Looks like the mist is beginning to clear. Fill me in please on what is stirring the pot."

"Well, first of all, you are definitely stirring the pot, but Beulah's trip to the police has definitely added some salt and pepper as well as some garlic and onions. I think some old memories that have been long hidden are stirring and rattling her. I don't know if that is your doing or whether that's just the reason that she decided to see you."

Tucci leaned forward and said, "You are my best source of inside information. What do you think is happening?"

"I think her loneliness is stirring things up for her and making her more aware of her bland existence. She doesn't see her daughters or grandchildren much, and the Merry Mags, who used to be a lifeboat in her school years, don't keep a lot of contact. They all have their own families and lives. I'm sure your approach is opening some windows as well."

Tucci sat back in his chair. "You came out to talk to me today. Tell me what's on your mind."

"Well, all this business with the police, with our dreams, with maybe someone being killed, and with people following people, is definitely stirring up all kinds of feelings in all of us. I would like Beulah to get some answers as to what the hell is going on. She doesn't know if it is this life, a past life, or whether she is just plain nuts, and as a result, she is complicating things."

Tucci had a whisper of a smile, looked at her with a glint in his eye, and said, "All of us? How many of you are there?"

Ruth's pattern of smile wrinkles emerged. "You old fox, Dr. Tucci. Of course you surmised there were more than the two of us. There have been several over the years, but most have outlived their purpose and do not show up much anymore. The young child who retreated into a curled-up fussing toddler, for instance, and the angry and defiant teenager have managed to sort of grow up. Rarely do any of the others show up anymore. I end up taking care of most of what their antics provided."

Tucci looked at her and said, "And you know it is unlikely that a previous life is what we are looking at here, but repressed memories of things that occurred in an earlier part of this life. Of course, you might remember a lot of those things, because you would have been occupying her consciousness during many of those events. She was using you to protect her from painful feelings. It was good of you to help her out."

"Do you work with the police, Dr. Tucci?"

"I have consulted with them at times in the past, but only in pre-arranged cases. I do not provide them with private information from patients unless the person I am working with specifically requests me to do so. This has not happened in my practice. The only exception would be if I was aware of an imminent threat that the patient was planning to harm someone. In my forty years of practice, it has never happened."

She glared into his eyes. "Then it's safe for me to talk to you about Eddie and the Merry Mags?"

"It is confidential, and it may answer some questions as to why these dreams and memories are cropping up now. "

"Then what more do you want to know about Eddie?"

"I know that he is dead. Is there more that I should know about that? It was something that you avoided when we met earlier. I assume the details around that are stirring things up."

"Well, you did have that dream about him during my first session. How weird was that? That certainly stirred the pot."

"I was definitely picking up vibes from you. I don't know how I do that, but it happens from time to time, and it is usually something important when it does happen. They were your vibes, though, and my intuition tells me they are important."

Ruth puffed a sigh of resignation. She sat looking like she was trying to sort out where to start. She grimaced a little. Her fingers played with the wedding ring that she still wore as if she was pondering about where she should start.

"I suppose I should start by talking about Eddie, but I think I should tell you a bit about the Merry Mags. They are tied in with Eddie, and they were the best friends I had at a time in my life when I needed friends the most. I already told you about my sexual experiences with Eddie. Now I guess it's time to go into some of what happened afterward."

Chapter 11: Merry Mags

Ruth looked around the room with a slightly vacant stare, as though she was struggling with where to start.

"The Merry Mags first became acquainted through pain, suffering, and empathy. Some of us were pretty, some were not so pretty, some were shy, some outgoing, but we were all rather naïve and unassuming. Most of us were eager to fit in and to be accepted, as most high school kids are. We were generally ripe to be dazzled by boys who showed us much attention. For some, it was the first time that boys showed us any real interest. For others who might have been seen as more attractive, it didn't matter that much, because every time they looked in the mirror at that age, they saw all their own faults. Maybe one ear was higher than the other or a birthmark made one feel conspicuous. Another might feel self-conscious about some acne. There was always something to be uncomfortable about. Kids at that age were always looking in the mirror."

Ruth paused as though she were perusing events in her history.

"I think the real startup of the Merry Mags began on that day that I found Emily crying in the bathroom. She was not the only one who worried about pregnancy that year and who was dealt with poorly by some of the boys. Some were lucky, like me, not to get pregnant. I was fortunate enough to have a means of escape, or better yet, retreat from the rage that I sometimes felt. I had my daytime dreaming, as Beulah, to back away from my feelings, but that left a lot of the anger to fester in me, as Ruth. I guess I began to engage with some of my classmates as Ruth, this fun-loving gal who could tell bawdy stories as well as anyone on a given day, and who could be this clueless sweetie, as the day-dreaming Beulah, on others."

"So, what led you and your classmates to being able to climb out of your personal pain and finding a way to put away your personal embarrassment to interact with each other?"

"Like I said, the beginning for me was the day I met Emily. I watched what unfolded for her, and it almost killed her. I wanted to do something, so I began to watch the other girls, and I picked up on the pain that I could see happening for some of them with various boys. I decided to make friends with those that I could, especially those that I thought of as 'outsiders', who were not pretty or outgoing or generally 'popular'. Basically, they were loners trying to fit in but who were particularly vulnerable to predatory boys. Several of us became friends who hung out together. We were essentially outsiders who had put together our own inside. Then as Emily healed and came back to school, she joined us, and some of her cheerleader friends would saunter in and out of our group. We didn't have a formal pact of any kind, but we helped each other out a lot. That's pretty much how the Merry Mags got started."

Tucci sat back. "Wow, sounds like you put together a group of self-supporting friends, but it sounds like it probably became more than that, or it would not be stirring up a lot of angst for Beulah."

Tucci was quiet for a moment. Then he said, "Is Beulah aware of Ruth? Does she know that Ruth exists? Or any of the others who reside there within her – past or present?"

"Most of the others don't know each other. I never thought it would be a good idea or there would be too much confusion and squabbling."

Tucci took the moment to reposition himself in his chair, leaning forward slightly as if to invite her to tell him more. Getting her attention, he said,

"Ruth, maybe it would be best if those who still live there got to know each other and learned enough about one another to help each other out like the Merry Mags did. You could support one another, coordinate your behavior, and it could reduce confusion. It might prevent getting yourself into predicaments such as the one with the police. After all, you all live in the same house, so to speak, and if some trouble comes your way, you are all stuck with having to live with it together, sooner or later."

"And how am I supposed to do that?"

"Maybe by letting some of the memories in bit by bit. Maybe by recalling some of the better memories of the closeness with the Mags at first, like we did by talking about your daughters, and easing into some of the rougher stuff. I think you would know how to do that. I am guessing that you have been monitoring that kind of stuff for years without really realizing it, only in reverse, keeping it out of awareness."

Tucci backed off a bit to let these ideas sink in. They both sat in silence for several minutes.

"Do you think you are ready to let Beulah have an awareness about that part of her that is you?"

"I think I need to do it gradually, Doc. I am having enough trouble just putting it together for myself. Is it OK if I do this on my own timing?"

"Yes, I think that is the best way to approach it. You know you better than I do, and it's going to work best by you figuring it out."

"Dr. Tucci, I am feeling emotionally spent. I think I need to stop for today. Can we continue at our next appointment?"

"Good idea, but a little advice – have Beulah hold off with the police until she is more fully aware of details of her past, so she is fully informed about what is factual and what her limited awareness has her believing. Now put your head back, close your eyes and let Beulah join us, refreshed from her restful nap."

In a moment Beulah opened her eyes, smiled, and said, "Uh oh, I guess I dozed again. I'm sorry Dr."

"Don't be concerned, Beulah. It was a heavy session, and I think I wore you out. I'll see you again soon. Go home and rest."

He watched her slowly use the arms of the chair to push herself upright, reach down to get her coat and slowly put her arms into the sleeves and adjust the collar. She did look drained. She looked at him with peaceful eyes and said, "Thank you, Doctor. Same time next week?"

"You bet, Beulah. Get some good rest and have sweet dreams. Call if you need to."

Chapter 12: Tucci's Secret Life

After Beulah left, Tucci remained in the office thinking about where this whole process was going. The reality was that he didn't really have that much to go home to. Like Beulah, his kids had left the nest some years ago. Teresa, his wife, had been a wonderful companion. They enjoyed music, theater, and ballet, and made time to enjoy the outdoors. With a busy psychiatric practice, getting away for extended periods to travel was not easy, but long weekends at the coast were refreshing, and a day boating on the river was delightful. The easy companionship shifted about four years ago when Teresa had a stroke and deteriorated rather rapidly. Within a year she was gone and the struggle to make sense of the rest of his life emerged. They had met when he was twenty and had been together for forty years and married thirty-eight. "Keep busy!", he told himself. "Take up old hobbies." Ultimately, he found himself immersed in his practice. Doing the things that he had enjoyed doing with Teresa was not the same when doing them alone. He took up photography for a while, but after finding that he was taking hundreds of pictures, and they all seemed to remind him of places he had visited with Teresa, he began to lose interest in the repetition. There was dinner with friends, coffee with friends, playing cards with friends, watching sports, TV, whatever, but it didn't quite fill the void. He had to keep his mind busy. He gravitated to books. Nonfiction grabbed him - stuff about science, interesting people, nature, things that distracted him, yet filled some gaps, but reading was still time alone. Hypnosis had intrigued him from the time of his early training in the field. He had read numerous books on the subject and had incorporated it into some of the work in his practice. He did not advertise using it. He didn't want to accumulate people who wanted him to hypnotize them to quit smoking or eating too much. He found it useful, however, to help anxious people learn to relax and to distract from irritable but persistent symptoms like tinnitus. It was also quite useful as a tool in working with Multiple Personality Disorder. These patients seemed to be especially susceptible to suggestion, and thus to hypnosis.

He sat in the chair perusing his office. He didn't often sit at the desk across the room unless he was writing a report or doing research. The Monet print soothed him. The books on the shelves were dusty. It was the people he treated who kept him alert, aware, alive. He thought about Beulah. He wanted to know more about her parents, especially her father and his impact on Beulah. Were there similarities between her husband and her father? She had not talked about either of them much. When she had, the way she talked about her husband had literally put him to sleep. He also had to know much more about the Merry Mags. Was she still in contact with many of them? He thought about his own buddies from his military years and how they continued to support one another through the years.

He looked at his watch, stared at the Monet for a few minutes, and wondered what he would get to eat. "Italian? Chinese? Something soupy with noodles, I think." That seemed to be his life now, wondering which waitress is working this shift at which restaurant, what the soup of the day might be, or whether to just go get a beer and chat with whomever is at the bar. He got up, locked up, and left.

Chapter 13: Introductions

Tucci anticipated one of two responses from his ladies after their last session. Either Beulah would present herself tightly wrapped so that her emotions found it difficult to leak out, or she would be more relaxed and relieved. Instead, he was surprised.

"Dr. Tucci, now I know why you fell asleep during one of our earlier sessions. I was boring the hell out of you. I was going on and on about my husband but not really telling you much about what he was really like. He was a lot like my father. Both were old school and rather rigid. My father grew up in the depression as did my mother. He insisted on being the rule-maker in the family. My mother's opinions didn't count much on the surface, though she had a way of slipping them in under the table, so to speak. Dad was quite protective of me. You might call it hovering. You might have surmised that I never told him about my sexual exploitation by Eddie, for my protection as well as to prevent the hullabaloo that would have occurred if he had found out."

She stopped and pulled a tissue out of the box next to her and wiped her angry tears. Her lips were curled. "I was afraid of him. He wasn't a very good dad." She sat for a moment frowning.

"My husband, George, never found out either, for a while. He probably would not have married me, had he known. When I eventually told him about it, he became quite angry, both at this person Eddie, as well as at me. Things were quite strained between us for quite a while after I disclosed that. I was sorry that I did, especially after Eddie's death. I found out that there are some things that should just stay secret. I guess I should apologize for holding back with you, but I think it boiled down to not really trusting you yet." There was still anger in her voice, but anger at herself.

There was another pause. Then Tucci said, "It looks like some of what we talked about last time has had an effect. What else have you been able to pull out of your magic hat?"

"Well, for starters, Dr. Tooch, you have been the magician here. You have enabled me to look at my life more objectively, almost as if I were watching a movie. I am beginning to see my relationships within my family in a different way. And with my friends as well."

"No, Beulah, you are the one who came to me for answers. You were looking for something. You just didn't quite know what. What you needed was someone to point you in the right direction. I showed you where the stones were, but you did the work of rolling them out of the way. You didn't know yet what you were looking for, and probably don't fully know yet, but it looks like you're ready to pick it up. Let's have at it."

Tucci's statement was like a starter gun in a race.

"Let me start by telling you about the dream I had the night of my last appointment. It was not a wandering daytime dream, but it was a vivid dream during my sleep. It was as though there was another person in my body. She called herself Ruth. She recalled incidents in my life that came back into my awareness. Before the dream, I had only been able to vaguely recall snatches of them. Yet, they became quite vivid, and I know they were real. It felt to me like this Ruth person was my guardian angel helping me out. Does this sound crazy to you, Dr. Tucci?"

"Not crazy, Beulah, but the protective part of you coming into your awareness to help you without having to keep you in the dark. You see, Ruth has also decided to let me know about her presence in your life, and she has taken my advice to let you know about her, so you can work together. She is a part of you."

"So, you knew about her? Why did you keep it from me?"

"She spoke with me the last time you were here – like one of your daytime dreams. I thought it best to let her introduce herself to you. Looks like she chose a night-time dream to do so."

"So, some of the things that happened did not occur in a previous life, but were kept hidden from me?"

"I cannot tell you that a previous life does not exist, but I can tell you that I have seen individuals who have experienced some of what you have experienced, sometimes starting at an early age. They may take on different roles at different ages to fend off things or people who appear threatening. When I see that happening, I find it best to help all of the so-called 'alternate personalities' to become aware of each other and communicate with one another for the common good. They sort of 'all live in the same house', and if something bad happens to one, it happens to all."

"It makes me angry that this was kept from me."

"So, who are you angry at? Me? I'm trying to fix it. Yourself? You were doing the best you could to protect yourself with what you knew at the time. You can learn to do it better. You just need a guide with a compass to point you in the right direction. Let me say that you are progressing quite well so far. Why don't you tell me a little more about what you and Ruth talked about in your dream."

Beulah gave a big sigh and sat quietly for a while. Then she spoke. "My head is in a bit of a twirl. I've been thinking about the Merry Mags a lot lately. Mind if I talk about them?"

"You are the guide. You have done well so far in that capacity. I'll trust you to keep me on the path."

"Back then when the Merry Mags started up, it was very gradual. It was at the end of my second year in high school that I met the first of the gang. I told you about Emma, the cheerleader and how we sort of started up. By the end of summer and into my junior year, I had kept my eyes and ears open and had been aware of other classmates who had had bad experiences with boys, and I began to connect with several of them. It was mainly for support, but after talking about our experiences, we began to fantasize about getting even. As our group got bigger, some girls began to act on some of these ideas we talked about. One of these was a friend, with whom I still connect from time to time, named Lisa. We nicknamed her 'Loosey', not because she was sexually loose, but because she didn't keep a tight lid on her temper. She was one smart gal, got good grades and put her brain to good use. She went to the public library on her own and figured out a lot of anatomical male vulnerabilities that she sometimes put to use. She even took jiu jitsu classes for a while and encouraged a few of the Mags to learn it with her. Boys didn't mess with her much after that."

Tucci looked at her with a slightly tilted head and a raised eyebrow. "Sounds like a force to be reckoned with. Did she ever get into any trouble with her temper?"

"She got close a few times, but ultimately, she knew when to quit. She really did have control, but she looked enough like she didn't, that people knew when to back off."

"Did the Merry Mags as a group ever get into things that could have gotten out of hand?"

Beulah thought for a bit and nodded. "There were times when someone could have gotten hurt, and there were a few times when someone did, but it was usually cleaned up without a major incident. Some of these are still a bit fuzzy in my head, but I can see glimpses of them from time to time. Some are still like those daytime dreams we talked about."

"Please tell me more about your husband and what happened when he found out about your encounters with Eddie. Did he know about your connection with the Merry Mags?"

"John was furious with me for not disclosing that I had been sexually active with someone else before we married. He looked like he was close to reaching out and hitting me. When I saw that, I was reluctant to tell him about the Mags, thinking he would blow that all out of proportion as well. He insisted that I tell him who it was that ruined my virginity. He insisted that I tell him, or he would divorce me. I wasn't sure how to handle it, and I told him. I thought he might kill Eddie, and for all I know, he might have been the one who eventually did so. It wasn't too long after Eddie was killed after a bar fight that John seemed to settle down. We never talked much about it after that. We never talked much about anything of import after that."

"It sounds like you have led a rather lonely life, other than the friendships that developed through the Merry Mags. What ever happened to the high school boy with the job who was too busy to engage much socially in school? Whatever happened to him?"

"Yeah, he was a nice kid. I think he eventually became a marine."

There was silence for what felt like minutes. Tucci knew the power of silence and waited to let it all digest. Beulah's eyes perused the room, taking in the bookcase, the desk, and landing on the Monet.

She finally broke the silence.

"I don't think any of my fears were about things that happened in a previous life. I think they were related to things that were confusing because of the mess up in my mind's way of dealing with things. What I need to do is to straighten up my understanding of my past and to look ahead to what I want my life to be."

Tucci smiled at her. "I think your mind is doing a pretty good job of sorting some of these things out. I'll continue to act like the poles on an alpine ski course that guide you to keep within the course, but you will be the one needing to make the turns and staying on your feet. You are showing me that you can do it. You are smarter than you thought you were. Let's call it a day and give your thoughts more time to settle. I'll see you next week, or sooner if need be."

Chapter 14: Kraft Back at it

Detective Kraft continued to grind away at his murder case. There were not a lot of new clues. The victim was single, in his mid-thirties, owned a small jewelry store that was financially in the black, had no criminal record, and he wasn't known to be a gambler. There was no known recent girlfriend, though he had dated a woman up until about six months prior to his death, when she had moved twelve-hundred miles away to reunite with an old boyfriend. In his youth, the now dead man was known to dally with several young women and a couple of older ones. Apparently, they got tired of what they perceived as a lack of commitment, and he would find his way to move on. Kraft was able to track down a couple of his dalliance partners and spoke to one who admitted to meeting him for several secret trysts in a relatively secluded location. She had subsequently divorced her husband. Kraft looked long and hard at her as a potential suspect, but she had a strong alibi. She was out of the state visiting her mother around the time he was killed. She did not give a very favorable picture however, of the character of this man. The other woman that he knew had had some doings with him did not want to talk to Kraft about him, but she was glad that the guy was dead. Apparently, there were a number of people who held some animosity toward him, but no solid leads for Kraft.

This continued to direct Kraft back to Beulah. There was nothing solid there, either, but her approaching the police, her familiarity with the area, and her peculiarity in general was enough to keep him thinking about her. He felt the need to find a way to get her back in to see him so he could find out more without frightening her off. He thought about getting Tucci to encourage her to talk to him, but he knew that was hopeless.

Tucci would never engage in that kind of chicanery. He settled, finally, on the idea of calling her in for more information on what she saw in the area when she was visiting there, since she had had such a visceral experience there.

Kraft made the call. He was surprised that he caught her at home on the first try.

"Ms. Blanche, hello. This is Detective Kraft. I am still working on that case involving Mr. Frank's death. I am trying to fill in some holes in our investigation, and since you are familiar with the area where we found the body, I would like to go over your impressions of the place as you experienced them when you were there. Would you be willing to come and speak with us again about what you experienced there?"

"Well, Detective, there's probably not much more I can tell you other than what I told you the last time."

"We just want a fresh look again. Sometimes when a little time passes, things pop up that might have been missed from previous conversations. Could we arrange another meeting?"

"I guess it wouldn't hurt to think about it some more and come in to talk about it. When would you want to meet?"

"How about tomorrow? Would morning or afternoon be easier for you?"

"I'll plan to come by about ten tomorrow morning if that is Okay with you. I presume we'll meet at the same office where we spoke last time."

"That would be fine. I will look forward to seeing you at ten. Thank you."

Kraft was pleased that it went as smoothly as it did and hoped tomorrow would go as well.

On the following morning, Beulah somehow felt stronger. Her last conversation with Tucci had bolstered her in a way that surprised her. She suspected that Detective Kraft might be looking at her suspiciously. Why else would he be calling her to quiz her again? However, she did not feel the need to be fearful with Tucci in her corner helping her to understand herself. She decided to wear a dark pantsuit. Somehow it allowed her to feel more confident and in charge of herself. As she strode into the rather bare-bones police building and saw both Sgt. Barnes and Detective Kraft waiting, she noted their take on her appearance. They both seemed almost startled at the air of confidence she seemed to exude.

"Good morning officers, I hope things are going well for you today." Beulah was radiating charm. She knew that Sgt. Barnes was going to join them so that Kraft would have a witness in case anything of import should happen to spill out. They shook hands and meandered to the same room they had used before with the metal table and chairs.

Chapter 15: Memories

Going back into the stark interview room gave Beulah goose-bumps. It felt cold with the metal desks and chairs and the linoleum floor. The walls were bare. She was suddenly fearful, but she covered it well with her smile as she presented a positive attitude. She hoped this new discovery within her, Ruth, would help guide her through this query. She knew that she had nothing to do with the murder that was being investigated by Kraft, but she feared memories related to incidents from her past that might pop up and implicate her in something else that, as for right now, she had no immediate recollection. Tucci had stirred up some anxiety about her spotty past with the Mags, and her lack of memory of details was a little unnerving.

Kraft was careful. His approach was gentle. He leaned back in the metal chair and tried to look like it was comfy. Sgt. Barnes did likewise, but they both looked pensive.

"Beulah, I am up against a wall in trying to solve the case of Mr. Frank's death. That was the name of the man that was found dead in the area that you were birding. He apparently owned and operated a jewelry store in Benton County, but for some reason was stabbed to death in Pierce County, which is some distance from his residence. Yet, in your dreams, you seem to have some means of being aware of some of the details related to his death. For example, you dreamt about where the body was found, the kind of wounds he endured, and incidental things about the place like the salamanders. Have you ever known yourself to be clairvoyant?"

"No, Mr. Kraft, I have never been aware of any prescient information or experienced any kind of clairvoyance that I can recall. I have had a lot of weird dreams that Dr. Tucci thinks are my way of escaping from uncomfortable situations. I'm not always sure of what I am escaping from, because the dreams seem to keep me from remembering what I have been up to. Sometimes I remember parts of the dream; sometimes I have a kind of amnesia for what I have been doing."

Beulah's mouth was getting dry. She did not want to get into telling him about the Merry Mags. Lisa did not want to be followed or interrogated. She had been clear about that. Beulah did not know whether Lisa had ever done anything that could have got her in trouble back in their younger days, but she wouldn't put it past her and did not want to drag her into this mess. She fanned herself and said, "It's a bit warm in here. Could I have a glass of water?"

Kraft looked at Barnes, who got up and left the room to get some. While Barnes was gone, she looked at Kraft and asked, "Have you gotten any new leads on this case?"

Kraft looked at her with what she surmised to be some suspicion. "We've been able to put some information together, but no definite leads. With the amnesia that you mentioned, can you jog your memory about whether you had ever before been to that riverside place that we spoke of last time? You seem to have had a rather vivid experience about that place. I couldn't help but wonder if the lack of memory could be one of those things that Dr. Tucci spoke about as a means of escaping."

Sgt. Barnes returned with a bottle of water. She took the opportunity to stop and drink a bit before answering Kraft.

"I really have no recollection of ever being there before. In fact, I had to do a bit of research to find the right road to get to that spot. If I ever do come up with any other memories about it, I will certainly run it by Dr. Tucci, and if he thinks it is important, I'll share it with you."

"Would you mind at all if I had a conversation with Dr. Tucci about your experience?"

"I would prefer that you not do that. I need to spend more time with him to understand myself better, and I would prefer discussing my private interests with him before he discusses them with you, if at all."

"Of course. I meant if something came up that you wanted to tell me. He might then be able to help me to understand the psychology behind it better. By the way, the man who was killed was from Benton County, and as I mentioned, his name was James Frank. He owned a jewelry store and was not married. If you happen to think of or come across any incidental information about him, it might be helpful with our investigation."

With that, she tightened, but shifted in her chair as though to preparing to get up.

"Well Mr. Kraft and Sgt. Barnes, if that is what you wanted from me, shall I be on my way? I'll be sure to get back to you if anything comes up that I think might be helpful to you in solving this case. And oh, by the way, that nice man that you have following me and taking notes --- he's probably not necessary, and frankly, a waste of your time and money."

Kraft grinned at her and said, "Thank you, Mrs. Blanche. It's very kind of you to make the effort to come back and assist us in this investigation. I hope you won't mind if something comes up that we might like to discuss with you again."

"I'll be happy to help the police with this in any way that I can."

Beulah slowly got up from her chair and walked out the door. She felt relieved but was not quite sure exactly why. The air of suspicion was a bit unsettling. She felt the urge to connect with Lisa to talk about her experience. When she got out to her car, she called Lisa.

"Lisa, when you get this message, please call me. I was called to talk to the police again. We need to talk."

Chapter 16: Looking Back Again

Beulah met Lisa for coffee the next day. They were careful to go to a small lunch spot situated in a shopping center, so that it would appear they just happened to meet there. By this time, they were both concerned about being observed by the police. Lisa started the conversation.

"Okay, kiddo, what's up? What did the cops want from you? I warned you about not giving them information about Eddie or the Merry Mags. All that has nothing to do with whatever they must be investigating."

"I didn't say anything about either of those things. I just had a weird experience in a place, it turns out, that just happened to be a murder site. They seem to be very interested in that experience. I've been talking with my psychiatrist about my memory lapses over the years. You know what I mean. The Mags teased me a lot during our time together about how I seemed to forget things. My doc thinks that those lapses were ways I used to protect myself from scary things. In fact, he's made me aware of parts of me that took over when I was off in dreamland. I didn't tell the police about any of this except that I sometimes have daydreams that interrupt my memory about stuff that is going on."

Lisa looked at her with those eyes which commanded attention. Her face was a mixture of glowering and smiling, warm but stern.

"I don't want you to talk to the police about our younger days. They have nothing to do with the present. Stuff happened with the Mags that we need to let lie. Nothing will change anything that happened back then. If it's not in your memory, leave it back there."

Beulah was perplexed. She knew that her curiosity would continue to pester her until Ruth pulled memories out of her. She looked at Lisa and said, "What do you know about what really happened to Eddie?"

Lisa paused. Her face wrinkled. She knew from her experience with Babe, that this question would persist until she got an answer or would keep trying to find the answer from someone else, and maybe the wrong person.

"Babe, your husband killed Eddie. We knew after you told him about having been raped, he was very angry. We knew he had a temper, and we didn't want him to hurt you, so some of us got together and told him where Eddie was hanging out. We all felt scared and guilty after it happened. We thought he'd confront Eddie, but we didn't think he'd kill him."

"Did you see him do it?"

"No, but we knew it had to be him, and after it happened, we could see that he lightened up. You told us that after Eddie's body was found, he seemed to let go of the whole thing, and he quit pestering you about it."

Beulah watched Lisa's face as she asked, "He was stabbed to death, wasn't he? There were mixed reports about how he died."

After a pause, Lisa said, "My husband's friend worked for the police back then. I asked him about a year ago how Eddie had died, since there were mixed stories about his being beaten, shot, or stabbed. He told me that Eddie had been stabbed numerous times in the chest and abdomen with a very thin blade, like an ice pick or something like it.

How did John react to Eddie's death at the time?"

"He seemed to settle down. I was relieved. The pressure fell off for me, but it was still there to some extent. The trust for both of us was gone. I didn't really feel relaxed in our relationship until John died."

Lisa looked at her with that impish twinkle in her eye.

"Just how did John die, Babe?"

"He was complaining of a strong stomachache and went to bed early. He died in his sleep. The doctor said it was a heart attack."

"Do you think it was something he ate?" Lisa watched for a reaction.

Babe brushed the question off and said, "No, the doctor said that sometimes a heart attack starts out feeling like a stomachache."

Lisa let Babe's answer go. She wondered, but let it drop. "Babe, if the cops call you in again, don't get into the Mags. Some nasty stuff happened back then, and it would not be good for them to be looking into any of that. They'd probably try to connect it to whatever they are looking at now."

They finished their coffee and went their separate ways. Both were a bit unnerved. Lisa felt rattled that Babe was beginning to recall stuff that, in the past, had been put out of her awareness. She had always been naïve and tended to blurt out whatever came into her head.

Now Babe was dreading the fact that she may have been involved in things that were perhaps rather cruel, and yet she did not remember them, at least for now. Eddie's death by a thin instrument like an ice pick was much too similar to that of the man whom Kraft was investigating.

Lisa's questions about John's stomachache before his heart attack began to gnaw at Babe, raising questions that she perhaps might be involved beyond her memory. Things between her and John were quietly rancorous toward the end as they orbited around each other.

This meeting, instead of clarifying things, left both women unsettled.

Chapter 17: More Introspection

Tucci had been gone for a week visiting his family. Beulah began to wonder if she depended on him too much. She missed not seeing him. When he returned in time for her next appointment, she was ready, or so she thought. She wanted to travel back in time, to her earlier years, as though she was going to a previous life. She told Tucci about her meeting with Lisa, and how it set off bells for her. She wanted to know more of what her memory had suppressed.

Tucci looked at her and said, "So why do you want to know the things that may have been so painful that your mind protected you from them?"

She sat upright in her chair and looked him in the eye. "I want to know my life, what I did, what I said. I want to grow up and stop being afraid."

He looked at her sudden intensity. It was a new look that he saw. She looked younger than in his previous encounters with her. "You're not looking very afraid right now. Did something happen that set off a new resolve in you?"

"I had another encounter with the police. They called me in again to talk, and I am sure they have someone tailing me. I also met an old friend from high school. Meeting with her got me thinking more and more about those absent memories. Some of that stuff feels like it's not that far from the surface. And the dreams with Ruth continue. I want to know myself better, even if it causes me problems."

Tucci looked at her seriously, but with a glint of a smile. He was concerned but recognized her growth. "Perhaps Ruth is helping you with the growing up process that you want. Perhaps she is going a bit slower than you'd like, but maybe she's afraid to pour on too much too quickly. What are some of the stirrings that you see just below the surface? I can see that they are uncomfortable, but I also see that you have mustered up some strength to deal with them head-on."

"The dreams with Ruth are still a bit vague, but I had a conversation with my friend Lisa that, once again, brought on those old feelings about being responsible for someone's death. This time it was more direct, and I began to wonder whether I had something to do with my husband's demise. It clearly would not have been in another life, but if at all, would have been in another aspect of this life, and now I can see where that could be a possibility."

Tucci saw an opportunity. "Perhaps we should call on Ruth to come out and give us her perspective on these issues. However, if she comes out to join us, I want you here too, perhaps like a mouse in a corner, while she and I talk. Then I'll invite you into the conversation when I see that she is ready, and you are ready to carry on together. Are you comfortable with that kind of a get-together?"

Beulah had that befuddled look. "How do we speak to each other when we're the same person?"

Tucci smiled and said, "It doesn't matter. The important thing is getting to know each other better and listening to what each of you thinks. You'll see. It will come to you. Are you ready to give it a try?"

Beulah nodded.

Tucci dropped his voice and said, "You know the routine. I want you to relax and close your eyes, but instead of going to sleep, I'd like you to rest but stay alert to what Ruth and I are talking about. I'll ask you to join us when we are ready. So, for now, please close your eyes momentarily and let's have Ruth join us."

She closed her eyes, and her chin went to her chest. It took about thirty seconds for them to open again, and Ruth said, "Do you really think she's ready for this, Doc?"

"We're about to find out. She's here and listening and I have confidence that she's strong enough and ready enough to handle it, and you have been watching her grow, so you know it too. Let's start by your telling me about your husband and about his death."

"You mean HER husband, Dr. T."

"No, I mean YOU plural. You were all together in this even though Beulah said the nuptials. Better get used to that idea. You all need to be clear about that for starters."

Chapter 18: Days of Our Lives

Tucci looked at Ruth. "So, tell me more about your husband. His name was John, but what did you call him in your day-to-day dealings?"

"I called him John. Early in our courtship and our marriage, I tried to be affectionate with his name, calling him sweetie or cutie, but he was averse to that, and I realized that he just preferred to called John."

"Was he affectionate in other ways?"

"He didn't show much affection openly. He was clearly uncomfortable doing so. He did the usual compulsory spouse stuff, like getting me a card on Valentines Day or my birthday, but never in a public display. Looking back, he was clearly a stuffed shirt."

"What drew you to him?"

"He was what there was. He showed me some interest. He was sort of affectionate when we weren't around other people. I saw him as shy but caring. I was not exactly a magnet for the opposite sex as far as my physical attractiveness. I felt fortunate that he had an interest in me, and he generally treated me kindly."

"Doesn't sound very romantic."

"It was what it was. It could have been worse. I learned to find excitement in other things, like my kids. I still kept in touch with some of my friends from the Merry Mags."

"How did he find out about Eddie?"

"It slipped out one day when we were talking about whom I dated in high school. We had been married for six or eight years, and I thought it was safe to talk to him about that. It clearly was a mistake."

"What happened?"

"He blew a gasket. He was angry with me not telling him about it before we got married. He said he felt cheated. We didn't talk to each other at all for days, and only when necessary for a few weeks after that. Then we found out that Eddie was killed by someone, and he seemed to let go of his blatant anger, at least. We never talked about Eddie after that, but it always simmered in the background."

"Sounds like it took quite a toll on your marriage."

"It was never ideal, but it was never the same after that. We sort of co-existed. When John passed away, I was both sad and relieved. I was startled recently by something my good friend Lisa told me. She said that she and several of our Merry Mag friends had assumed that it was John that killed Eddie. The thought blew me away, but John was gone, and there was no way to dig it out of him, if you don't mind the pun. It made me think more of my idea that I might have been responsible for someone's death."

"And the idea of this happening in a previous life?"

"It's becoming more obvious now to me that my so called 'previous life' probably has more to do with my dream life that we have been talking about lately."

"Maybe it's time to bring Beulah into this conversation a bit more. What do you say Beulah?"

Ruth did not fall asleep but suddenly changed her expression to one of wonder.

"Doc, this is a lot to take in. It's a lot different from waking from a dream or watching a movie. It's more like seeing a play on the stage with real people in the parts."

She paused. "It opens several other doors to what seems to be just hallways. How is all this connected to my birding experiences and those dreams about finding a body? And all the questions raised by detective Kraft? But most of all, how many parts of me are in me, and how do I keep control of what I know or what I do?"

"That's exactly why I connected you with Ruth. That's the starting point, so you can be aware of all that makes you, so you can become one person. It's a start."

"So, was my first thought about what was going on with me correct? Am I crazy? Am I some kind of schizophrenic?"

"You're not schizophrenic, Beulah, but you have developed what I refer to as a means of protecting yourself from things that you feel might harm you. If I were to put a label on it, it's called a dissociative disorder. It used to be called 'multiple personality disorder, because different aspects of one's personality tend to show up to deal with different issues. That's when dreams, as you call them, tend to happen, usually after a fear is encountered. It's as though the right hand doesn't always know what the left hand is doing or did. To help that, it's important for you to get to know each other and be aware of what the others are doing. That's why I felt it was important to start with you becoming aware of Ruth."

"You mean I could have done things that I have no memory of?

"Memory is there. It's just been kept from you. That's the reason for getting you to know each other, so you all know what's going on."

After a long pause, Beulah glared at Tucci and asked, "Is she still here? That Ruth person? I want to know why she kept me in the dark for so long. I'm pissed at her! She had no right to keep me in a closet all my life. I have a right to know about my life and what I know and what I feel. I feel like she's kept me in prison."

"She is part of you, Beulah. You live in the same house, your body and your mind. Like the others, she just showed up one day to protect you. Both of you are looking for help. That's why you came to me in the first place. That's what you want, isn't it. It's what it is, but it can get better, and for what it's worth, you're stuck with getting to know each other as roommates now and there's no way around it."

"Shit!"

There was a long pause. Tucci didn't know whether Ruth would pop out again, or if Beulah would stay. He hoped it would be the latter. When he saw tears, he knew it was Beulah.

He said, "It's like a jigsaw puzzle. Looking at a pile of pieces doesn't make a lot of sense until you put them together, and then you begin to see the picture."

"This is hard, Dr. Tucci. Why are you doing this to me?"

"I'm not doing it, Beulah, I'm undoing it, so we can put it back the way it's supposed to be."

With another sigh of surrender, Beulah looked at Tucci and said, "Okay, Dr. Tooch, do what you do best."

It turned into a long session. Tucci decided to have Beulah listen to Ruth tell him about the various alter personalities and how they arrived in the picture. There was a little girl who was described as curling into a little ball when she felt especially threatened and a teenager who sometimes acted more like an aggressive boy when the need was felt to defend Beulah. As she grew older, a rather stoic part of her emerged, who backed out of confrontation with others and withdrew. Some personalities worked better than others.

Ruth also realized that she was the most effective at keeping the peace and making things work. She persisted, because she was the most consistent, but she knew it would not work forever, so she had made it a point to get in touch with Tucci.

Ruth paused, got up, walked over to the water pitcher and poured herself a glass. She knew the Merry Mags were something that Beulah was more familiar with. She described them to Tucci as a good bunch of supportive friends over the years, even as they surpassed their high school years. She and Beulah continued to keep in touch with some of them. They had all been tight knit, sometimes in tough circumstances.

Tucci decided to have Beulah join into the fray and began to involve her in the conversation as well as Ruth.

"Beulah, did you ever have any memories or pieces of familiarity when you came out of the daytime dreaming that you did when you were with the Merry Mags?"

A distant recollection began to emerge on her face.

"I vaguely remember an incident when I recalled slapping someone across the face, but I couldn't remember who it was or what it was about. It was one of those times when I was coming out of one of those daytime dreams. I remember being in tears and my friends were hovering around me trying to comfort me, but I don't remember the details."

"Were there other times when you had snippets of memory like that?"

"Maybe, but those memories didn't stick around for long."

"When you were in school, how was your memory there – in your studies?"

"I was always good at math, and I liked nature and art. Science was interesting. I enjoyed art classes and literature. I really enjoyed painting and photography. For some reason, I was especially attracted to abstract art. I saw stuff in those works that surprised me. It's like I could explore the artist's emotions. My parents never liked it when I came home from school with what they called scribbling. They would ooh and aww when I got a high grade in math, but I would find my artwork in the trash from time to time."

"Do you continue to do any painting or sketching?"

"I haven't for a while. It would be interesting to take it up again."

"May I suggest you do that? I would love to see some of your abstract work and have you talk about it to me in a way that I can understand and appreciate it. Maybe it'll help me know and understand you even better."

"I will give it a try again, Doc, but this has been a long session, and I am really tired. Can we wind up for today and give me a chance to soak this all up before our next visit.?"

"Sounds like a plan. Same time and day next week? Get a good rest. I'll see you both again soon. You know you can always call if you need anything sooner."

Chapter 19: Art as a Portal

When the ladies arrived a week later, Beulah brought with her a painting she had been working on. It was quite abstract, but Tucci could see that the setting was like a mist or fog with an open area one could perhaps be walking through to see a hazy outline of a menacing hulk of some kind. The colors were dark and gray with splashes of red as though in disarray. When Tucci asked if she could comment on the work, Beulah replied, "It's hard to explain a feeling. It's both frightening and exciting. It's as though I am going to find out something important when I get through the fog, but it's scary."

Tucci looked pensively at her work with his whisper of a smile. He spent several minutes peering at it from different angles and distances. His first comment was, "Marvelous!", and he continued to gaze at it. "If you could utter the first word that comes to mind, what would you say?"

Beulah blurted out the word, "Blood!" Then she said, "But there's some light beyond that mist."

Tucci held up the painting again, gazed at it longer, and said, "Yes, I see it. And I agree, it could be scary, but I also see the excitement in it. Please tell me more about what comes to mind."

"For some reason I feel fear but also anger, as though I must pierce the fog to confront something. The fear seems to come from some kind of threat, but the anger tends to overpower the fear."

"Is there a person or thing that brings out the anger?"

Beulah looks at Tucci quizzically. "Eddie, of course. --- And my husband --- And my father."

"Have you been thinking about Eddie recently? Or dreaming

related to him?"

"Over the years I have often thought about Eddie. I wondered how he had died. Was he shot? Was he it over the head with a bottle? Was he stabbed? Was it a drunken brawl or did someone have it out for him and just killed him? Did it somehow have to do with me? Sometimes I felt sorry for him and how his life veered off the road. Other times I felt the rage at how he had altered my life and that of others."

"Just how did he alter your life?"

"Well, he took my virginity! Being used by him made me aware of my mediocrity, my lack of attractiveness. It led me to choosing to marry a man I really wasn't in love with, just to fit in and have what I thought would be a normal life. At the same time, I never got back the excitement I felt at having someone see me as appealing and desirable. I locked myself into a relationship that was mediocre at best, and it numbed my sense of self. It kept me from expanding my options, my life."

"So, Eddie not only interfered with your sense of self but also briefly allowed you to see through a window of what it could be, and then it came crashing down." Tucci paused a bit.

"As bad as he was, maybe it was not all bad for you. For a while it allowed you to see yourself in a positive way. Now that Eddie is gone and your husband is gone, does it give you a different view through that window?"

"Unfortunately, my time for excitement seems to have passed. I'm an older woman now. The thrill of romance has dissipated. My fear of having caused someone's death still haunts me, but not like it did before, when I thought it happened in a previous life. Though some things may have actually happened in my alternate life. What they were exactly, I'm not sure of. Somehow, though, in my work with you, I'm finding a different kind of excitement. I am seeing myself behind the curtain like in the Wizard of Oz, and it seems to be waking something up in me."

"Yes, and you still have a life to live. It's not over till it's over, and you seem to be in good health. The impediment of living with people that might hinder you is no longer there for you. The gateway in your painting, like your life, is open, even if uncertain."

"Yes, but being alone is not easy. As much as it was difficult to be at ease with my husband, he was company, and we did things together sometimes."

"I do understand what being alone is like, but remember, being alone does not always have to be lonely, yet it certainly takes some sorting and planning to make it work for you. Things can change – for the better or for worse. For example, you seem to be going through some change. I find, today, that I am not sure whether I am speaking to Beulah or to Ruth. It's as though you are both here without my having to specify to whom I wish to talk. I am thinking that the fusion of your personalities is beginning to happen. Positive change is taking place. If that part of you is coming together, other parts of your life can change for the better as well."

Both sat quietly for a few minutes. Tucci wanted to give her time to let all of this sink in. He didn't want her thoughts distracted away by other questions until she had time to digest what he had just suggested. After a while, Beulah brought up the painting.

"It was exciting to get out my paints again. It makes me think and feel at the same time. I even had the fantasy that once my feelings become more clear, maybe my painting will become less abstract.

"That's an interesting thought. Feelings are important, though. It's important to be able to identify them enough to not let them interfere with what we think."

Another pause.

Tucci looked at Beulah and could see that she was tired. There was a lot of information to digest, and he thought perhaps this was enough for today. They arranged to meet again in a week, with the proviso that it could be sooner if necessary.

Chapter 20: Still at it

Detective Kraft persisted. There was not a lot of new information to go on, but bits and pieces seemed to fall out of his inquiries like seeds when you're squeezing oranges for the juice. Like jigsaw puzzle pieces, they didn't make a lot of sense until you got enough together to start to get an idea of the picture. For example, he found out that the area by the river where the murder had taken place was known to be frequented by local teens as a swimming hole and a place to party. It had been a favorite place for a rendezvous as well, off and on over the years. The elderly teachers he had interviewed were well-familiar with it. The weapon used was most likely the bloody ice pick, but a police dog scouring the area for clues also happened on a single blue topaz clip-on earring that was not damaged by weather. "Not a lot to go on." Kraft mumbled. He was still puzzled about Beulah. Her experiences at the murder site were uncanny, but there was no direct evidence of her being involved in the crime itself. He continued to try to track her as best he could, but so far, it was fruitless. When he checked with her about the earring, she denied having anything like it, and said she did not like clip-ons. She also told Kraft that she would not have dressed up to go birding.

Kraft was beginning to feel like he was approaching a dead end, but on one of his forays with the older teachers, he picked up on a rumor about a group of women, in their forties now, who referred to themselves as the Merry Mags. Curious, he dug into it a bit more and found they were originally girls who banded together for support. Digging into it a little more, he found they had sometimes gotten into some trouble at school for being a bit too aggressive. Once some of them had gotten a couple of boys drunk, and when they were tipsy enough, managed to beat them up a bit. That caused a bit of a ruckus with several sets of parents. Kraft decided it might be worthwhile to follow up on whatever happened with these vigilantes. Curiously, he discovered that Beulah had belonged to this group, and incidentally, the woman she had visited at the mall had also been a member. It seemed just a little too much of a coincidence for Kraft to let it pass. He began to look a bit more into Lisa's past. In the local library, he discovered that copies of the local high school yearbooks were kept year after year. He scoured over them. Lisa Barnes's name came up frequently in Beulah's years. She was in the drama club. She was noted to be proficient in some form of martial arts outside of the school, which at that time was not something girls got into very often. There were photos of her and of Beulah together with another group of girls. The photos of this group made their appearance in several of the yearbooks of that era. When Kraft quizzed his older teacher friends, it was apparent that Lisa Barnes was quite a luminary in that group of girls. Since Beulah continued to be in contact with her, he thought it best to keep her in the equation and to find out what he could about this group of Merry Mags.

Chapter 21: Another Angle

Lisa Barnes was uneasy. Since Babe had visited her and told her about her visit to the police, she had the feeling that someone was tracking her. In her last call to Babe, she warned her about getting too folksy with the cops. She remembered how she and the others had gotten close to big trouble in high school, and she did not want to bring any of that old stuff up now which could stir the pot. She didn't have a clue about this guy who got murdered, but with Babe's tendency to let her mind wander and forget things, she hoped it wasn't Babe who was involved with him. She apparently did have some weird experiences where the guy was found. Also, Lisa never was sure whether Babe was in on Eddie's death. She always suspected it may have been Babe's husband. He was such a jerk, but no one cared because it was Eddie, after all. As she thought about it, she wondered whether Emily the cheerleader could have been in on it. She didn't do well after she healed from her surgery. She always looked depressed after that, and she never married, but she had family members who were quite angry at Eddie.

Lisa found herself muttering, "Why am I going off in my head about Eddie? He's long gone. But he's a big part of why Babe is who she is. And now this shrink that she is seeing seems to be stirring up all kinds of things. Is he putting thoughts in her head? Is she somehow involved in this murder in that swamp by the river? God, I hope not."

She decided to get back in touch with Babe. Much as she saw Babe as a bit muddled, she was a friend and Lisa cared about her. She also didn't want her to spill the beans about anything that might still get them in trouble.

She also decided to check in on Emily. It had been about a

year since she had run into her, and she wasn't looking great then. Maybe some clarity would dribble out of all this stuff. She set it up at a restaurant where they could have some privacy without a lot of lunchtime clatter. Linda arrived first, but Emily was not long after and waved excitedly as she came in. They caught up on all the latest family issues, latest books read, latest movies seen, and friends they had caught up with. Lisa brought up Beulah.

"I've run into Babe a couple of times. She's got a new man in her life."

"She does? Who?"

"Well, it seems to be other than a romantic liaison. It's a psychiatrist."

"Oh my God! I'm seeing a shrink too. Best thing that's happened to me. A year ago, when I saw you, I was down in the dumps and couldn't seem to shake it. I was referred by a friend and found this guy to be kind and attentive ----- and intuitive. He's not pushy but slides me into telling him what I'm thinking, though I often didn't know I was thinking it."

"She's seeing some guy named Tucci. Seems that she really likes him."

"Oh, Lordie! That's my shrink too! No wonder she likes him. He's a great guy and a great shrink. I'd like to get together and compare notes with her. I think I'll give her a call."

Lisa jumped in immediately. "Better yet, let's all three of us get together. I'd like to know more about this shrink stuff too. Maybe I could use a little straightening of my own warped mind. Shall I call Babe and see what we can set up?"

"Yes, let's do that. I'd love to connect with her again. She was always kind to me from the time we met in the women's bathroom."

They finished their coffee and agreed that Lisa would connect with Babe and set up another get-together. As Emily sauntered off with a big smile on her face, Lisa speculated about Tucci and the changes he seemed to have effected in both of her friends.

Chapter 22: Reconnection

They met for lunch in a quiet corner of Lisa's favorite deli. It was a late lunch, so they could avoid the noon crowd. Their excitement was palpable. After hugs and a bit of chatter, Emily got right down to it.

"Lisa tells me that you have a new man in your life."

Babe giggles and says, "Well not exactly. I started seeing a psychiatrist."

Emily grins. "I know. Lisa told me. I'm seeing Dr. Tucci too. I have been for about a year. He's been really helpful getting me back to living my life again. Do you like him?"

Babe smiles. "He's incredible. He's not pushy, but he gently digs in and gets me thinking about things that are in my head but aren't organized. It's like we're on a tandem bicycle and I'm in front steering, but the direction we're heading depends a lot on which way he happens to be leaning."

Knowingly, Emily relates how she has been able, with Tucci's help, to get out of reminiscing about her past struggles and mistakes and to get on with her life. "He's been a Godsend. He's helped me to see the opportunities for better choices without outright telling me what they are. He leaves it up to me, but he encourages me to have the courage to go ahead and do what I know I need to do."

Babe hesitates, then says, "There is also another man in my life, but in a different kind of way." She goes on to talk about the police, Kraft, the birdwatching experiences, the murder investigation and how it may be turning into more than she had bargained for. Yet Tucci seems to be helping her to sort this out as well. "The Tooch, as I like to call him, has helped me to remember things in my life that were apparently hidden away in my mind, and it seems to be awakening my spirit. I feel like I'm healing, much like what you seem to be doing, Emily."

Lisa comes into the conversation once she is able to get past the excitement of these two who have not seen each other since they've embarked on their shrink adventures. "This whole thing about the police worries me a bit. We dodged a few bullets with the Merry Mags back in the day. I don't want to dredge any old stuff up this late in the game."

Emily frowned. "Why are the police so interested in us?"

"Babe went to them originally to inquire about murders or deaths or accidents or something. She was having weird dreams and was spooked about something she thought she may have done. Enough was said that they were curious, and because she happened to be birdwatching where the body of a murdered guy was found, they were especially interested. Then we happened to get together for coffee shortly after, so now they are traipsing after me as well."

They talked about the murder for a while. Lisa had read more details about the victim in the paper. When Emily heard more, she realized she also had heard rumors about him from friends. There apparently was suspicion that he had been involved in some way with moving drugs. The three ladies were curious enough that they decided to pursue the rumors without, hopefully, attracting suspicion to themselves. The police seem to want to talk to Babe from time to time, and maybe she could quietly pass on what they have found. They agreed to meet again in a week or two to see what they could find out, but mainly just to get together again.

Chapter 23: A Fresh Start

Beulah came to her next appointment with Dr. Tucci with a different sense of comfort. She felt somehow more relaxed. Along with her new sense of freedom, she brought with her another painting. It was a scene looking through a window at a beautiful woodland with a small creek surrounded by wild daisies. She proudly showed it to Tucci. He smiled and said, "Wow, you've expanded from abstract to quite naturalistic. Quite a change in a short time. Nice work."

"I met with a couple of friends. I may have told you about Lisa, the friend from high school that I had coffee with. The other is my old high school cheerleader friend who was pregnant with Eddie's baby. She is doing much better than she was the last few times that I saw her. She tells me that she is happier because she happens to also come to you for help. You didn't tell me that you were seeing one of my Merry Mag pals."

"And I didn't tell her that I was seeing you. Does that surprise you?"

"No. It's really nice to know how private you've kept me. I was thrilled to see how positive she was about life. She seems to have put aside all the grief she carried and now seems grateful to be living. It made me think of my journey with you as well, and how my perspective has been changing. When I look at myself in the mirror now, I don't see this plain unattractive person that I used to be. I see a mature woman who has grown confident in herself, and I know you are a good part of that."

"I'm glad for you, but I want you to know that you were ready for who you're becoming, and you've been willing to explore and sort things out and work to get there. Give yourself some credit. I am just a catalyst."

"Things do seem to be changing for me. My friends call me by the old nickname they gave me – Babe. I'm beginning to see myself as Babe instead of Beulah, and I like it. It's like I'm waking up to myself for who I am, not who I used to be."

"Would you like me to start calling you Babe instead of Beulah? Would it better fit your newly developing persona?"

"Actually, Dr. T., I would like that, if you don't mind, at least here in the office."

"On another note, when you look back over your various experiences, do you ever see times that you've been quite angry?"

"Actually, Dr. Tooch, I don't see anger as much as fear; fear of not being accepted, fear of being rejected, fear of being ridiculed. I remember being irritated at times, but I was too fearful to be outright angry. It's probably what resulted in my other parts coming out to help me escape from uncomfortable situations."

Tucci smiled. "It's comforting to awaken to a new kind of awareness of yourself. With this new look at yourself, are you still concerned about having been responsible for someone's death?"

Babe frowned. "I don't know what that was all about. Could I have known about something that I was somehow aware of in one of my dream states? I can't imagine myself actually hurting someone on purpose. Whatever that feeling was, it led me to contact you. I'm grateful for that. There's only so much I want to recall about some of the weird things I may have done when I was sort of outside of myself. I want to know who I am, but I'm more interested now in knowing who I can become."

She paused a bit, leaning back and scanning the office. The desk, the bookshelves, the Monet print, the funky chairs, all had a homey look to her. She was comfortable. It was not just because Tucci was there. She realized how calm she had become with herself.

Tucci let the pause continue for several moments. Unlike

in the past, Babe seemed quite relaxed sitting in the quiet office with neither of them speaking. Too much silence from the shrink would usually loosen the tongue of a patient and get them talking, but today, all was quiet.

Babe eventually began to talk about her kids. She had begun to make more phone contact with them. She was animated when she talked about taking a trip and paying each one of them a visit. Tucci inquired about whether detective Kraft had continued to be in touch.

"I haven't spoken with him in quite a while. I wonder how he is coming in his investigation. My friend Lisa seems to be concerned that someone is keeping track of her whereabouts since we had coffee together, but he hasn't connected with me lately. I wonder if he's making some progress."

"Have you been having any of those daytime or nighttime dreams lately?"

"You know Dr. T., it's sort of strange that I haven't had any of those episodes since I got acquainted with that part of me that is Ruth. I am now recalling things in my past that I had either forgotten or had blocked out. They don't bother me much. I sometimes say to myself, 'oh yeah, I remember', and I feel some relief that my memory is coming back."

"Any memories that scare you?"

"Not really. I think Ruth is still doing her job of keeping that kind of stuff out of reach for a while yet, but I'm not feeling afraid. Actually, I'm feeling kind of excited. I feel like I'm coming alive again."

She paused. "I am having some strange dreams lately, though, that don't seem to be related to anything else. I frequently dream about salamanders. It's as though they are vying for territory between one another. They're each trying to get to the top of a small mound of dirt. One manages to get there, but soon another pulls it off and scrambles up. It's been rather repetitious."

Tucci smiled and asked, "Had you ever thought that the salamanders might be symbolic of other events happening for you?"

Babe looked at him quizzically. "What could they be symbolic of?"

"There are aspects of your different personalities that, at times, seem to be wrestling to be out there in front."

It was as though a light bulb turned on for Babe. She giggled out loud.

"Of course!!"

They continued to talk about the changes that Babe was feeling for another ten minutes or so. Tucci couldn't help but note the evolution in Babe's demeanor.

"What say you, Babe. See you in a week?"

"Sounds good, Doc."

Chapter 24: Another Old Acquaintance

Emily had arranged for the three ladies to get together again for lunch. She said she had a surprise for them. "I'm bringing someone with me that you would never guess I ran into." When they queried her about whom she was bringing, she said, "Never mind. You'll see when we get there." The intrigue brought both Lisa and Babe to the café early. When Emily and her guest arrived, neither of them recognized him. He was about six feet tall, lean and fit, and about their age. He carried himself with confidence and an air of gentleness and was casually dressed.

"Gals, I want you to meet an old high school classmate. This is Clark Cooper. He left our high school and joined the marines. After he retired, he took a job with the state police, so now I call him Cooper the copper. I ran into him after a fender bender."

Lisa laughed and said, "Who bent whose fender?"

Emily grinned. "Some guy smashed into my car at a stop light, and he happened to be someone that Clark was investigating. Apparently, the guy was wanted for questioning by the police for another matter, and 'detective' Clark was on the case, so we ended up talking and made the connection."

Babe grinned. "I remember you, Clark. You were always friendly, but you would always disappear after school when a lot of us would hang out."

Clark smiled. "It's nice to see you all again. Yeah, high school days were a while ago. I remember you all. I was kind of shy back in those days. I remember you tended to hang together, and as you got older, you gave some of the guys a run for their money. Especially you, Lisa, you didn't take shit from anybody.

You had me scared half to death."

Lisa grinned. "Oh, come on, Clark, I wasn't that bad."

He still had a boyish smile. "You definitely had that look about you."

Lisa knew it. She had perfected 'that look' over the years. It had come in very handy at times. "So, what are you working on these days, Clark?"

"Well, I've been working with a variety of things over the last couple of years, but John Kraft has asked me to help him out with a couple of cases down in this part of the state, so I popped on down."

They caught up for the next hour, recalling sports events, snowstorms, teachers, and various students. Eventually, they began to talk about those classmates that were no longer alive, and the subject of Eddie came up. Clark's circumstances during that high school era were such that he didn't have time to mix much with other students in social events, but he was very much aware of the questions surrounding Eddie's death. As far as the police were concerned, it was still an open and unsolved case. Because the similarity of both Eddie's death and that of the most recent murder, Kraft had begun to look at a possible connection between the two and had requested Clark's help on the case. He surmised that Clark had known Eddie, though somewhat peripherally, and that he had a sense of what it was like to be in that environment at the time.

Clark had been a smart kid in high school. He'd gotten good grades. He'd stayed out of trouble generally. He hadn't dated girls much, though he had secretly had a bit of a crush on Lisa but was too shy to pursue her. He thought it a bit of a stretch for Kraft to connect Eddie's murder with that of the more recent one, but it gave Clark the opportunity to visit his old digs after a long hiatus. He remembered Eddie well. He'd never liked him much and wasn't particularly surprised at how he had eventually died. He saw Eddie as popular, not because he was likeable, but because he was flashy, outgoing, and a successful athlete. He wasn't particularly smart, and when he wasn't trying to charm the ladies, he could be a bit of a jerk.

Lisa found herself surprised at how she reacted to meeting an old schoolmate whom she had barely noted when they were high school classmates. She found herself suddenly feeling flirtatious and had to hold it in check.

"So how long have you been back here in this part of the state, Clark? Have you been missing your roots? Do your parents still live in the area?"

"Well, my parents passed on while I was stationed at the embassy in Spain. I made a quick trip back for their funerals. They had died suddenly in an accident while they were on vacation, so it was a hurry up thing, and I had to hastily take care of their business before I returned to my duties. It didn't give me much time to visit."

"What about other family?"

"My wife died of cancer a couple of years ago. We never had kids, unfortunately."

He let the conversation drop at that point, and the ladies offered token sympathy, but the blush of interest was clearly aroused in all three.

The conversation began to wane. People made excuses about having to get to other things. They made open plans to get together again soon and gradually departed. Clark insisted on paying the bill. As she stood up to leave, Lisa said, "I'll pick up the tab when we get together again. How about next week, same day, same time?"

Clark looked up and smiled and nodded. "I'm in." he thought to himself.

Chapter 25: Flashbacks

Babe returned home to an empty house, but it didn't feel empty. The afternoon had been fun. It felt a lot like the old days when the Mags would get together and have a lot of laughs. The thrill of meeting up with Clark surprised her. She flashed back to a memory of him as a teenager, standing in the hallway at school, looking a bit bewildered. He had transferred from another school and was trying to get his bearings in new surroundings. She had directed him to the correct room for his class, and he had thanked her and smiled kindly at her. His shyness was obvious. Her interest had been piqued, but her focus at the time was on Eddie.

Lisa also had left the meeting smiling. She remembered viewing Clark as being aloof, but at the same time, shy and unavailable. The fact that he was now a police detective made her feel wary, but he seemed pleasant enough and seemed to enjoy the ladies' company. The fact that he, too, was single, made him more intriguing.

Emily was proud of herself for finding Clark and bringing him to the group. The afternoon left her with a warm sense of memory for the good times gone by, but also with a glow for this newfound friend. She remembered him in high school as being appealing, but at the same time as insular and unavailable.

Clark felt quite fortunate to have connected with these women so quickly. Part of his task in coming down to help Kraft was to mingle with old connections and to gather up any information that might be helpful in putting the pieces together. He too had memories of those times, not all pleasant. He particularly had an antipathy toward Eddie back then, whom he saw as a bully. On one occasion he had happened upon Eddie taunting a younger student in an empty hallway. Clark was tall and lean, but strong. He told Eddie to leave the kid alone. Eddie continued to harass the kid. Clark had had enough and grabbed Eddie by the collar and screamed in his face, "I said to leave him alone!" Eddie withered and walked away. He tended to keep his distance from Clark after that. For Clark, it wasn't surprising that Eddie had eventually met a violent fate.

Clearly this chance encounter had stirred up feelings in all the participants. Both Emily and Lisa were surprised by their own intrigue and interest in Clark. For Babe, it stirred up other feelings that she could not pin down, at least until she slept that night.

Babe's night was restless. She dreamt that she was talking to Ruth in her sleep. They were walking side by side, as though they were separate people, strolling along the river where she had dreamt about finding the body.

Ruth looked at Babe and said, "I remember this place. Eddie brought you here once in his parents' car. I think this is where he raped you."

Babe was startled. "I think you're right. It's also where I found the dead body in my dream."

Ruth had an impish smile. "Do you think the two are connected? This is our dream, you know. It must mean something to us."

Babe startled awake. It was time for tea with a shot of rum. An hour later, she was ready for another go at getting some sleep. As she dozed off, Ruth was again there at her side and said, "Those goofy salamanders are at it again."

Babe looked at her and said, "You know full well what those salamanders are doing. By the looks of things, some of the others want to come out and join our conversation. Is this your doing, Ruthie?"

"I can't say it's not an opportune time, dear Babe."

A group of three seemed to emerge out of the misty bank of

the river. One was a child, another a teen, and a woman in her thirties. They all acted as if they were familiar with one another, the child hanging and pulling on the teen. The older woman had a reserved look about her but made it a point to tolerate the other two.

Ruth waved as they approached and said, "It's time we all got to know one another better. Beulah likes to be called Babe now. She knows of you, but her awareness has taken some time. It took her a while to understand that we're all together as a person and found different ways to handle things."

Babe suddenly startled herself awake again. She was shaking and sweating. Her mouth was dry. She found herself angry having to deal with these issues when she was half asleep and vulnerable. She didn't know if she was angry at Tucci or at Ruth, but she had come to Tucci for whatever he could do for her, and Ruth was just a part of her trying to put it all together. She wondered if the evening's get-together had triggered these crazy dreams. She stayed awake as long as she could and had some more rum. Eventually she slept again with enough rum that she was without dreams.

Chapter 26: Recollections

Over the next several days Babe found herself recalling snippets of events. Back in her youth there were no cell phones and teens tended to gather in small groups to chatter about events of the day. She had a sudden memory of hitting a boy in the face with a book, which would have been unlike her. She found herself chuckling about that. She also remembered a feeling of fear when her father had been quite angry and took his belt off to spank her. Now she just felt angry at him.

Then there was Eddie. A lot of her sense of shame and embarrassment that had been set aside came leaking out again. However, time had helped her with a different take on a lot of these feelings. She knew it was wrong to wish death on anyone, but she did find herself taking pleasure in what had happened to him.

Babe looked back at the past year and what had happened since she had started seeing Dr. Tucci. She realized that she had begun to look at him like a father figure, but a benevolent one. Her father had been rigid and strict, as was her husband, but 'the Tooch' encouraged her to find it within herself to grow. She smiled as she thought about how much she had learned about herself, and in such a short time.

A few days later, she arrived for her next appointment with Tucci. She walked in confidently, went over to the chair and sat down. "It's time we talked about my father. I've been thinking a lot about him lately. He was a gruff old bastard. He could be mean and nasty if he didn't get his way. His parents came from the old country, somewhere near Germany. They were definitely old school – 'spare the rod and spoil the child' kind of people. Dad didn't veer far off that path."

Tucci wasn't sure whether he was talking to Ruth or Babe. Their demeanor and composure were beginning to look a lot alike. He didn't bother to ask. He was pleased with the result. He smiled and said, "Where do you want to start?"

"First of all, he didn't really like to be called 'Dad'. He thought it was much too familiar. It had to be 'Father'. He had to make the decisions, he handled the money, and he decided where to go when we vacationed. At least my mother was in charge of the kitchen, once she found out which foods he clearly did not like. She seemed, though, to keep her emotional distance. On one occasion I noticed a bruise under her eye. She was serving us dinner. She stopped briefly, looked at him and said, 'If that ever happens again, you'd better not ever go to sleep.' He seemed to be less bossy to her after that, at least from the perspective of a seven-year-old."

"Did he ever hurt you, physically that is?"

"It became clear to me at an early age that if I was 'disrespect-ful' by talking back, arguing, disobeying, or whatever, I was in for getting my butt spanked. I also noticed over time that other people, even grownups, seemed to give him some distance. He presented a gruff and surly demeanor. I remember him always bringing a fancy-looking cane with him whenever he left the house. It was like a walking stick with a fancy metal handle. He seemed to have a special interest in it and would never let me or my mother handle it. After I was married and shortly before he died, he talked to my husband privately and passed the cane on to him, who also kept a tight private hold on it. That damned stick is still in my closet at home. I was so conditioned to leaving it alone that I just tend to avoid it."

"What was your husband like? Sounds like your father took a liking to him."

"Actually, my husband was a lot like my father. He wanted to be in charge. He didn't want me to work a job. He preferred that I stay home and be a housewife. He managed the money. He wanted to make the decisions. When I made the mistake of telling him about Eddie, he was enraged. He probably would have divorced me except that he would have to figure out how to deal with the girls. We operated at a distance for quite a while, at least until he found out about Eddie's death. Then things lightened up a little. We never really got comfortable. I never really admitted this to anyone including myself, but I was actually glad when John died. Yes, I was glad when he died, and I was glad when Eddie died. I can say it now." She had tears in her eyes.

Tucci sat for a moment, letting her feelings settle. Then he said, "You know what? We've been at this for a while, and I just realized that I don't know if I have been talking to Babe or to Ruth, or both. Which is it?"

She had a puzzled look. "Well Babe, of course." She looked around. "But Ruth is probably here too."

Tucci smiled. "I would guess that you are probably right about that. Maybe you've become so used to each other that you come across in a similar fashion, but she probably is here as well." He paused. "When you originally had the thought that you might be responsible for someone's death, did you have anyone in mind? Was it your father, John, Eddie, or someone else? Or was it a vague feeling?"

"Doc, I am not quite sure, but I'll think about it. I need some time to digest some of this. In the meantime, I have been having dreams of walking together with Ruth. It's pulled some memories out of me, and she's introduced me to some of the others apparently living in me. It's unsettling."

"From what I've seen of Ruth, she tends to keep a tight lid on things. I would trust her to maintain control so that things don't get out of hand. It sounds like a good idea for all of you to get to know one another so that you can support each other like the Merry Mags used to do. I would recommend that you get to know them. They are all parts of you. If you're frightened of the process, you can just walk along with them until you get to know them better. When you're more comfortable, you can try interacting with them. You don't have to do it all at once."

Babe relaxed. There was something comfortable about how this guy put her at ease by letting her go at her own speed. It was soothing to see that he never seemed to be rattled by the presence of these ghosts within her. For the rest of the hour, she excitedly talked about her two daughters. They arranged the time for the next session, and Babe left. Tucci sat for a while and stared at the Monet print. Then he wondered where he would get a bite to eat. "Chinese tonight, I think."

Chapter 27: Kraft and Cooper

Kraft had not known Clark Cooper for long, but he knew of his reputation. Both were with the state police and had offices in different parts of the state. Cooper had gotten out of the military after twenty years of service, where he had a well-established reputation for doing intelligence work. Kraft was looking forward to working with him. They had spoken numerous times by phone but were finally getting a chance to meet and put their heads together. The murder of the jewelry store owner was still a puzzle. There seemed not to be a financial motive. His business was in the black. He was not married but was known to be a bit of a philanderer. The possibility of a connection to one or other of the women he had dallied with was there, but nothing finite as far as tangible evidence. One of the women clearly had a thorn in her side about him but refused to talk to the police about it.

Beulah Blanche continued to be a part of the puzzle, mainly because she had inserted herself into it, even though she was like a piece that just somehow didn't fit. Yet her description of the type of blade that killed him was fairly accurate, but then it was just in a dream, and her discovery of the body was also in a dream. Cooper was brought up to date. Part of the plan was to have him peruse his old stomping grounds for information both new and old that might lead them in the right direction.

Cooper had kept his meeting with the three ladies rather low key and friendly. Yet he had the sense with them that there was a big scratch on the table that was hidden under the tablecloth. Meanwhile the women were impressed with him and none of the three were put off by his good looks and friendly manner. A week after their first meeting, Cooper arrived at the coffee shop as Lisa had mentioned, not knowing for sure if she or any of the other ladies would show up. He ordered coffee and sipped it for about ten minutes when Lisa walked into the shop. She waved at him and said, "Well, it looks like we didn't scare you off the last time. Glad you could make it."

"It takes more than three good-looking women to scare me off."

She smiled and noted that he grouped them together so as not to indicate that any one of them might especially appeal to him.

Within five minutes Babe and Emily also arrived. They chattered together for a while when Clark asked, "So what is in the works in this part of the state?"

Lisa looked at him and said, "Well Babe here seems to have become of interest to your colleague, Detective Kraft, for some reason. Maybe you can shed some light on that little tidbit."

"Oh, from what I know, Kraft is working on several cases. Babe came forward with information about the setting where one of the crimes took place, so Kraft wanted to get as much information as he could about the location. I believe the crime he talked about with Babe occurred in a county just north of here. Have any of you heard any scuttlebutt about it?"

Lisa popped out with, "We've just heard that the man was relatively young and in a business of his own – jewelry maybe? None of us knew him."

Cooper, with a smile, said, "I understand the area where the incident took place was in a secluded area that doubled as a rendezvous spot for younger people at times."

Emily piped in. "A bit too far north for a lot of us in our younger days. Most of the boys in our world were too cheap to buy gas to go somewhere exotic, like another county."

They all laughed. The conversation went on for another hour. There wasn't much further talk about the murder or the victim, but it was clear that these three widowed ladies had lightened up significantly while talking to a bright, successful man who happened to also be available. For a while the conversation shifted to older events that happened to be of interest to Cooper, such as Eddie's murder. He had been in the life of all three women in one form or another, and he had made an impression on Clark as well, in a negative way. He was intrigued with what happened to Eddie after he had left for the military. Cooper had looked at the record. Eddie had been stabbed several times in the chest with a long thin blade, but also several times in the groin, probably post-mortem. The last part about the groin wounds had been kept out of any public information.

Lisa leaned back and said, "Well, we managed to solve some of the puzzles of the world. Shall we get together again next week to have at it again?"

With a bit of shuffling, they gathered their things and went on their way.

Babe was surprised at herself. She didn't expect that she could again have an interest in another man. She didn't anticipate anything to come from it, but she seemed to feel her soul awaken again in her. Things have been changing in her awareness since she had been seeing Tucci. She was surprised that she was also having feelings of affection toward him, almost in a fatherly way, like he was taking care of her.

Chapter 28: A New Look

When Babe showed up at Tucci's office for her appointment, she brought with her another painting she had made, this time using pastels. It was a peaceful wooded scene by a small creek, accentuated by a variety of flowers and birds. The colors were soft but vivid.

"I thought you might like to brighten up your space here with some extra color, Doc. That wall right over there might be a good place to hang it."

Tucci smiled. "You must be a mind reader. I've been thinking about sprucing up this office a bit. These colors should just about do the trick. Thank you, and that wall should accentuate the light nicely." He went over to his desk, opened the bottom drawer, and took out a small hammer with some clips to hang the artwork. He had Babe help him to center it properly, checked it with her to make sure, and mounted the picture to the wall across from the Monet. They sat and admired the painting from across the room in the cozy chairs, as Babe liked to call them.

"Doc, I feel like my life is turning around. I'm not bored. I'm enjoying my painting like it's part of me again. I recently met an old classmate from high school that is an attractive man, and I find myself interested in him, even though I don't necessarily imagine us ever being a thing. The fact that I could feel that way at all is exciting to me. I don't seem to be doing any daydreaming, and I wake up from some of my night dreams smiling. I think my inner selves must be working together more smoothly. I don't seem to have that gnawing feeling that I may have caused a death anymore, though I'm curious where that came from. I guess what I'm saying is 'Thank You', but at the same time, I don't want to lose you, so please don't cut me loose."

"The interesting thing is that I never seem to cut anyone loose. I'm always hanging around, ready to jump back in. Usually what happens is that the people I work with find that they want to make it on their own at some point. They jump off the pier, swim out for a while, and swim back to catch their breath when they need to. I still occasionally connect with people who stopped coming in regularly some years ago. Sometimes a visit just helps them to ground themselves again. I welcome that."

They agreed to continue regular appointments but spacing them out a little further. For now, it would be every other week, but Tucci knew that he would let the spacing be up to Babe for the most part. He was pleased with her emotional growth. They talked for a while about her uplift in spirit, some of the things she was taking an interest in, like books, music, and even some sports. She had suddenly become intrigued with professional women's basketball. They set up an appointment in two weeks. She smiled at him and, obviously satisfied, sauntered out of the office.

He sat for a few moments looking about the office, settling on his new painting. He would think of it as 'Babe's Best'. He was glad to see her growing into her own person, not restricted by her upbringing or her controlling husband. The fact that she would consider an attraction to another man was a positive, since she never considered herself appealing to the opposite sex. It gave her an acceptance of herself.

Tucci's approach to any interest in another woman was different. His life had been full. He and Theresa had had their differences, but they had learned to accommodate each other's idiosyncrasies. He knew that to start over with someone else, it would be difficult to patch over his ingrained habits. He also knew that a pleasant companion might be nice, but the excitement of courtship and physical love would not be the same. He also did not want to start a relationship and not let himself get immersed in it, and find the woman had fallen for him. He didn't want to cause her pain if he didn't love her as much as she loved him. Then there was the issue of both of them growing older and needing care. Did he want to go through that? Tucci knew he was just making excuses, but he just wasn't there yet. Once again, what's for dinner?

Chapter 29: New Developments

Kraft was excited. Finally, there was some useful information. In going over sales records for the jewelry store owned by the victim, there were several records of transactions that didn't add up. One was for a set of blue topaz earrings. They would have been a match for the single one found at the site of the murder. The buyer was an elderly lady in her eighties who walked with a cane. When she was questioned about the purchase, she had no memory of doing so, and it was unlikely that she would have been walking in the area where the single earring was found. Kraft suspected that the store owner had 'cooked the books' in some way to cover up some shenanigans. The guy had a reputation for being shady with women, and he couldn't help but wonder if an angry husband or lover might have been involved in some way. Despite Beulah's weird circumstances, he was beginning to veer from seeing her as a viable suspect. They had found the weapon, a bloody icepick that was in the weeds at the scene. Beulah's description of a large hat pin could have fit the wound description, but was in her dream, and a lot of her evidence was apparently coming from her state of mind. Kraft began to focus more intently on the other women in this guy's life and the people related to them.

Cooper, in the meantime, continued to browse around and try to connect pieces back in his old neighborhood. He was intrigued with how things had ended for Eddie. He had never liked the guy back in high school, and he could see where he could have made people angry. He presumed that whoever had killed Eddie was furious with him about sexual issues because of the way his groin area had been butchered. As far as the murder that Kraft was investigating, the evidence seemed to be pointing in another direction, but Clark's curiosity had been whetted.

Then there was Lisa. She had taken a cautious interest in Clark. She was cautious because of his police connection. She had been involved in some shady behavior in the past and did not want him looking into any of that old stuff. Her friendship with Babe had always bounced from seeing her as a naïve kid to an astute and cautious woman. She was both amused and intrigued by Babe. As far as Emily was concerned, Lisa had felt badly about what she had gone through. She had always liked her but felt sorry for her. Now she was glad that Emily had managed to grow past the doldrums and get back into enjoying life. All in all, Lisa was enjoying their get-togethers and looked forward to more. They hadn't talked about Eddie much lately, mainly because of Emily. Lisa didn't want to bring up old memories for her. She wondered how much Babe really knew about what had transpired at the end for him. Lisa knew who killed him. She had helped to set it up. Babe had told her about the rape. She hated Eddie incessantly for that, and she knew someone else who felt the same. She tracked Eddie's whereabouts and hangouts. She knew when he went to his favorite bar and when he left it. She made sure that John, Babe's husband, knew what she knew. When she heard about Eddie's murder, she convinced herself that it had to have been John, and she was glad. She kept it to herself.

Chapter 30: Cleaning House

Babe left Tucci's office feeling refreshed. The fact that she had expanded her belief in herself was exciting. It was also nice to know that she didn't depend totally on the "Tooch", but he was there for her if she needed him. He really was sort of like a real dad. On her way home she decided to go through the old unused stuff and the memorabilia that had stacked up at home. She was ready for a fresh start. It would take some time and she would take her time, but she was ready to clean house. When she got home, she tossed her coat on a chair, put the teapot on and read some of the evening paper. When the water was hot, she poured herself a cup of tea, added some rum, and pondered the day's events. She was ready to start, but it would wait until morning when she was fresh. In the meantime, she decided to relax and do something she hadn't done in a long time. She picked up a book from the coffee table, curled up in her chair and started to read. She had always liked poetry. It was time for some Robert Frost.

In the morning, Babe started right in after her morning tea and corn flakes. She started with the books. John was a reader of what he called "serious books". He liked what Babe called "conspiracy theories", abstruse philosophical tomes, the bible, and some others that Babe didn't understand or didn't want to. She had picked up some empty boxes at the grocery store and began to glean the shelves. She had stashed several novels and interesting non-fiction books in the garage and brought them in. Babe worked up a sweat for a couple of hours and decided to shower. She would arrange later to have the boxed books recycled. She spent the rest of the day reading whatever she wanted from her stashed books. It was a gift to be able to sit and read for pleasure without John glowering at her for wasting her time. It had taken her a while, but she finally was ready to use her time as she saw fit without sensing his glare, even after he was gone.

On the following morning Babe decided to attack the closet. John had used one closet in particular for his "personal stuff". It was time to explore it. It was a walk-in room with suits, sport coats, pants, shirts, ties and shoes. As she took down the clothing, she checked the pockets, and sure enough, she found some stashes of money, a couple of twenties in one suit, a hundred-dollar wad in another. There was also a small address book tucked away in a corner. As she browsed through it, she noted the names of several women with their phone numbers. She tossed the book with disgust into John's pile for recycling. Then she spotted the generational walking stick that he had inherited from her father. Curious, she took it out of the corner and sat in a chair. What was so special about this cane? It was made of knotted wood that someone had cut in a forest. It was polished and varnished, and it was nice and well-balanced. There was a brass handle with a curved grip. It felt strange to be able to fondle it in this way. It was always his private item. As she looked more closely at the handle, she noticed an inconspicuous catch at its base. She popped it open, and nothing happened, until she twisted the handle about ninety degrees. Then it loosened up and the handle slid out with an eight-inch blade attached. Babe was startled. She noted some old, dried blood in a small crease. Whoever had wiped the blood had missed a spot. She thought, "Whose blood? Human? It had to be, or a different knife would have been used. Whose hand used it? John? Her father?" Stunned, she sat there for several minutes. She knew both men were angry individuals, but this she hadn't anticipated. Her mind went to Eddie. "Is this how he went?" She slid the blade back into the staff, secured it, got up, and took the cane to put back in the closet in a recess where it wouldn't be obvious. Not sure what she would do about it, she was clear that she wanted to clear out all the other unnecessary reminders of John in her life. She was increasingly aware of how fearful she had been of him throughout their marriage. "No more. I want him out! I want his stuff out – except for that cane!" She didn't know exactly why, but she knew she had to keep the cane.

Chapter 31: Elucidation Unfolding

Kraft continued to pour over the details of his murder case, focusing on the victim and his associations. Some of the retired teachers remembered him as a high school student and as having somewhat of a reputation for carrying on with more than one girl at a time. He was a good student but was prone to plagiarism rather than taking the time to do his own research. Kraft had been able to get a warrant to search his business and premises. He found a small photo album with various pictures of girls and guys, both from earlier times as well as more recent. He noted one photo that stood out for him. It showed a young woman in a bathing suit posing rather provocatively. What drew his attention was the fact that she was wearing distinctly blue topaz earrings.

Kraft's investigation refocused on the victim's romantic liaisons and ramifications. Using the photos, he was able to identify the lady in the picture with the earrings. As he sorted out her varied relationships, it was clear that her social life was complicated and included trysts with the victim as well as others. Things were messy in both their lives. It was up to Kraft to do some sorting. He informed Cooper about his discovery, but suggested they continue to keep an ear open to developments with Beulah and her friends.

After her discoveries from John's closet, Babe decided to call Lisa. She had frequently depended on her to help her think things through. Just as she had begun to appreciate a sense of equilibrium in her life, the issue of Eddie's murder had reappeared. Maybe she had been somehow responsible for his death. Maybe it had to do with something she said or did, not in a previous life, but in another one of her alternate lives. Ruth would have to help her with this as well, but she already had begun to feel as though she and Ruth had been melding. Then again, maybe Ruth was also unaware of whatever it was that happened to Eddie. Babe didn't want to talk about any of this with Emily present, so she arranged to meet Lisa that evening.

Lisa lived in a townhouse that was well-furnished. Babe had only been there a few times. It was on two levels with a kitchen, family room and dining area downstairs. Two bedrooms and a bathroom were on the second floor. There was also a guest bathroom and closet downstairs. Babe had always seen Lisa as a private person. They rarely met in the personal space of either. It was usually at a coffee shop, restaurant, or at an event of some kind. Babe was surprised that Lisa offered to have her come over to meet at her place. When she arrived, Lisa led her to the family room. It was cozy with a couch, two easy chairs, a TV and coffee table. Babe took off her sweater and sat in one of the chairs.

"Coffee or wine?"

"Red wine if you have it."

Lisa sauntered into the kitchen, opened the refrigerator and grabbed a wine bottle. "I like to keep it a little cool in the fridge once it's opened." She poured a couple of glasses and brought them back to the coffee table. "OK, Babe, what's up? You sounded upset when you called."

"What do you really know about Eddie's death? You told me once you assumed that John killed him. What do you really know about it and why did you assume that?"

"Whoa Babe! This is out of the blue. Where is it coming from?"

"I've been going through some of John's stuff, getting ready to clean out what I don't need. I've found a few stashes and some stuff that's got me thinking."

"What's that got to do with Eddie?"

"Among other things I found a small notebook with women's names and phone numbers. After years of his grumbling about my escapade with Eddie and not telling him about it, I find out he had several women on the side. What a hypocrite!"

"What's that got to do with Eddie's outcome?"

"That's what I want to find out. That's why I want to know what you really know about it. You always gave the impression that you knew more about it that you let on."

"What triggered this inquiry today?"

"I found his weapon hidden among his things."

"What kind of weapon?"

"It was a long, thin-bladed knife, but not the kind you would find in a kitchen. It was really a concealed weapon. The blade was carefully but firmly hidden inside the walking stick that he liked to carry around when he was out and about. I often wondered what was so special about that stick and why he was always so careful with it."

"What makes you think it was the knife that was used to kill Eddie?"

"It just fits. The way he behaved before, and then after Eddie died. You saw it. You said to me once that you thought he killed Eddie. And there was a trace of blood on the hilt that didn't get wiped clean. You don't use something like that to butcher an animal."

"Well, what if he did kill Eddie? It was over twenty years ago. John is dead. What's the point of digging up the past?"

"I am trying to piece together my life. I need to know what's real and what's made up. I need to know these things to start putting the rest of my life in order. I'm working with Dr. Tucci to do so, and things are starting to coalesce. Putting the puzzle pieces together helps me to do that. I know you're smart, and I want you to help me with what you've figured out."

"Well, Babe, I knew John was making your life tough, and I wanted to help you out. I knew he had to get it off his chest with Eddie and have it out with him. I didn't think he'd kill him. He knew we were good friends, and he approached me one day to ask me what I knew about you and Eddie. I didn't tell him much, but I knew where Eddie tended to hang out, and I gave him what information I knew. I thought they might fight. I didn't think it would come to more than that. When I read about Eddie in the papers, I knew it might have been John, and I decided to just keep my mouth shut about what I knew. You had enough on your plate without having to go through a murder investigation with John, and Eddie probably got what he deserved."

Babe listened to this and nodded. She sat quietly for a few minutes and said, "I wonder if I have to tell Kraft or Clark about this?"

Lisa leaned forward, alarmed. "Why would you want to do that? This is a dead case, if you don't mind the pun. Both John and Eddie are gone. There is no reason to stir it up again. It's not affecting anyone any longer. Emily is getting healthier. There's no need to stir it up for her. You are growing into your own person more every day with Tucci's help. Better to let it drop."

"You know me. Easier said than done. Maybe I'd better summon up the Tooch again to help me sort it out for myself."

"Please Babe, don't stir up mud again. People are healing. Look at Emily, look at you. It's fine to put the puzzle together for yourself, but it wouldn't help anyone to bring the cops into this again."

"Okay, okay, but I know that Tucci will keep it to himself." She knew that Tooch could bring out what she wasn't sure about by bringing Ruth and the others into play in his magical kind of way.

Lisa looked at her with sympathy. "I know it's healing for you, Babe, but don't scratch the scab too hard or the bleeding will start up again. Go ahead and talk to Tucci and let him help you get through this."

Babe knew Lisa was probably right. She agreed to keep it with Tooch, but she knew she would be calling him to set up another visit before their next scheduled visit.

Chapter 32: Revelation

Tucci wasn't really surprised to hear from Babe before their scheduled visit. He didn't mind arranging to see her between the set times. She was an intriguing patient who managed to come up with surprises but who also seemed versatile at handling them, and she was basically a pleasant woman. He essentially enjoyed his work. It was an opportunity to be with people, but Babe particularly piqued his interest. They scheduled another late afternoon-early evening time to fit her into his schedule.

She entered the office and gazed around the room. Her painting was prominently displayed on the wall across from the Monet print. She smiled. He pointed to the chairs and said, "You know the drill." Instead of sitting, she walked over to her painting and took it in. She looked at the Monet as if comparing the two, back and forth. She smiled again.

"Thanks. It's in a nice place, sitting there like it belongs with the other."

"In my opinion, it does." Tucci could be a man of few words when quiet was due.

Babe walked to the chair and sat down next to Tucci, who was already seated and ready for business. "I met with my friend Lisa to discuss some stuff I found among John's things. I thought about talking to the police about it but thought I would run it by her first. She's always been straight forward with me. We both thought it would be better to run it by you before making any decisions." She walked Tucci through the conversation she had with Lisa.

Tucci leaned back into his chair. "So, your friend thinks she may have inadvertently set Eddie up to get killed? Why would you want to go to the police with that? Both Eddie and John are dead. The murder case is essentially dead. What do you think it would do for either of you?"

"I'm just beginning to pull together the pieces of my life, but I feel like I want to know everything that other parts of me know. Working with you, I've begun to feel that Ruth and I are like twins but in the same body. I feel like we're beginning to think alike. I can't help but wonder if she knows more about John and Eddie. I thought I had put thinking about Eddie aside, but now thoughts about him continue to nag at me."

"You're afraid John may have killed Eddie. You have the cane-knife as probable evidence of that. You weren't aware of it at the time. You've discovered it years after both are dead. What other part of this is eating at you?"

"There's something about John. Somehow, I wonder if my demeanor, my attitude, my surliness toward John pushed him to the point where he wanted to take out his anger."

"I think it's time that you told me more about your relationship with John."

She poured a glass of water from the pitcher on the side of her chair, took some sips and leaned back. "First of all, John was very controlling. I grew to dislike a lot about him. Frankly, I was glad when he died. I didn't like living with him, but it would have been difficult to leave him. I really didn't have anything of my own, so I tried my best to make it work. It was a little better after Eddie died, but he really didn't change much."

"What was it about him that first drew you to him?"

"Well, at first, he was very gentle. He treated me like I was fragile. It was like he put me on a pedestal. When he found out about Eddie and what happened, I thought he would explode. He turned pale and I thought he was going to vomit. Then he got red in the face and was furious. He ranted at me for about twenty minutes. I was afraid of him. He was sullen and angry for weeks. When news eventually emerged about Eddie's death, he seemed to calm down, but his attitude towards me never really did."

"How and when did John die?"

"He's been gone almost three years. The coroner said he likely died of a heart attack. There was no autopsy or post-mortem investigation. He went to bed one night and didn't wake up in the morning. He had been sick, off and on for months, but his doctor never seemed able to find out what it was that was ailing him."

"What kind of symptoms had he been having?"

"He had some kind of a persistent cough and some short-ness of breath. He always seemed to be red in the face and com-plained a lot of having muscle cramping."

"Was he having chest pain?"

"Sometimes, but he wasn't eating well either. He complained about how everything I cooked seemed to have a garlicy or me-tallic taste. He pestered me to go out and buy new cookware. He said my cooking gave him headaches."

"What part of town were you living in?"

"We lived on the outskirts of town, out in the country."

"Did you have a municipal water supply?"

"No, we had our own well."

"How did the water taste out there in the country?"

"I thought it was terrible. I drank bottled water. John thought it was wasteful to spend money on 'such frivolity', but I ignored him."

"Did John ever have indigestion or stomach problems?"

"He often complained about stomachaches, but I tended to ignore his grumpiness and chalked it up to his complaining about my cooking."

"Did anyone ever warn you about arsenic in the water out there in that part of town?"

Babe startled and almost dropped the water glass. She was pale and sat quietly. "Oh my god! Was that what made him sick?

When we bought the house, they told us to get the water tested, because it was a new well, but we got caught up with other things and didn't get it done."

"A lot of the symptoms you described are some of the things that can occur with arsenic poisoning. Arsenic is tasteless and hard to detect unless someone is specifically looking for it. If you had been using bottled water and avoiding the well, that might explain why John was affected and you were not."

"So, whether I meant to or not, I had a lot to do with John's death. My time with Eddie and my time with John eventually led to their deaths. I told John about Eddie, and as a result, he died. And I let my anger at John ignore him, and he died."

"You can blow this all out of proportion, but the fact is that you led the best life you knew how to, and shit happened. Other people made some bad choices. Yours were pretty good ones. It's not good to take credit for someone else's choices. If you're wanting my advice, there are times to stir the pot and other times to let it simmer or turn the heat off. I suggest that you not take this back to the police. What's done is done. Why stir things up for your kids, or your friend Emily again?"

"What should I do with the walking stick? I don't know that I want to keep it around, but I'm not sure it's a good idea to just dump it somewhere."

"Bring it to me. I can keep it for you until we can work out what to do with it. It'll be safe here."

Babe took a breath. It was a temporary solution, but a relief. She could let go. They wound up the session and reset the appointment time a week out. She wasn't quite as ready to extend the time between sessions as she had thought. Meanwhile, they arranged a time for her to drop off the cane. She felt like Tooch had thrown her a life jacket. She wasn't out of the water yet, but she was safely floating.

Chapter 33: Quiet Time

Tucci quietly sat in his living room looking at the book he had just finished rereading. It was Shogun, a novel by James Clavell published in 1975. It had been fascinating the first time he had read it, and it didn't take him long to re-immerse himself into the samurai culture. The notion of seppuku or suicide as a way of honor intrigued him. He left his chair, went to the closet where he had put the cane that Babe had dropped off, and took it out. Sitting back down, he opened the handle and took out the blade. It was quite sharp. He wondered what Theresa would think of him if he joined her. He had been missing her sparkling laugh and smile. If he could be sure of an afterlife, he knew he would be able to join her, but he wasn't sure, and he knew there were patients and friends who would be shaken if he did. He knew it wouldn't be fair to them, and if he did join Theresa, she would also be upset with him for letting down the people who depended on him. The one thing that lifted him from his loneliness was helping people. As short-lived as it was, it did help. He put the blade back into the cane and clicked it into place. He mused about how an instrument that is used to help one navigate can also house something that could end the journey. The cane went back into the closet.

Television was definitely boring. Reruns were rampant. Tucci had thought he would travel more as retirement approached. Then Theresa died. Traveling alone did not appeal to him. To continue to have human contact outside of his practice, he had made a choice to join a writing class at the college. It gave him time to think, to put his thoughts into words and organize them. He didn't tell people about his profession at first. He didn't want to scare them off. Sitting at his laptop at home gave him the opportunity to immerse himself into an alternate world, or so he hoped. Sitting in a class with others gave him the opportunity to engage with them other than in a psychiatric capacity.

Tucci knew he should write about what he knew and experienced, but he had to guard people's privacy and remain confidential. He tried poetry, but it wasn't in him. He settled on brief anecdotes of people's fears, their pain, and their grief, but he tried to bring humor into his tales. In his training years, there was the man who thought he was Jesus and was sent to work at the carpentry shop at the hospital as part of his therapy. Another man feared the mafia was out to get him, so he refused to talk to anyone whose last name sounded Italian. This led to numerous humorous incidents. But ultimately, he wrote about what was familiar, his own experiences. Lately, that included parts of his time with Babe, but he disguised it to keep it cryptic. It helped to keep him alive in more ways than one.

Tucci realized that writing and his practice were not palliative enough, so he made a decision that he had pondered for a while. He decided to go to the local dog shelter and find himself a rescue dog, not a puppy, but an old timer like himself who could appreciate having a companion.

Tucci went the next day to the shelter and immediately spotted what looked to be about a three-year-old Golden Retriever. When he approached it, the dog bared his teeth at him. Tucci noted that his tail was wagging at the same time. The pooch was smiling. That was all it took. Tooch paid for his vaccinations and other fees and took him home.

Chapter 34: A New Co-therapist

When Babe arrived at her next appointment, she was greeted by Tucci's new companion as she walked in the door to the office. He wagged his tail, waiting for her to pet him. She had to chuckle.

"You have a new partner."

"His name is Sam I Am. Sam for short. He's my new co-therapist. You don't mind if he sits in do you?"

"Of course not, as long as he sits in and not on. He's a pretty good-sized puppy."

"He's pretty big but he knows the rules. He's a quick learner."

Tucci called the dog who immediately went over to his side.

Babe smiled. "I like dogs. I always wanted to get one, but my dad said, 'No way.' My husband was the same way. He said he didn't want to clean up poop or have to take a dog for walks."

Tucci scratched Sam's ears. "It's a lot easier when you're alone. Rather comforting too."

There was a pause. They always seemed longer to Babe than they actually were.

"I've been having more dreams this week since we met. They feel strange. They include both Ruth and another part of me who seems to act like a teenage kid. I hadn't dreamt about Ruth for a couple of weeks. It's like I didn't need to because we seemed to be on the same channel, but all of a sudden, this kid came into the scene. I think something about our last session must have triggered it."

"What happened in the dream? What did you talk about?"

"I don't remember how it started, but he was very angry.

When Ruth and I tried to calm him, he kept shouting about why we were letting John get away with murder. He was shouting and throwing things around and it got so loud that I would wake up, but after a cup of tea with a shot of rum, I would settle down and eventually go back to sleep. The problem is that I am running low on rum. The dreams continue to come. I've had several. They're all pretty much the same."

"Has this part of you been in your awareness before?"

"Only briefly several weeks back when Ruth introduced me to him and the child."

"What's his name? I assume he's a boy part of you."

"He goes by Rudy."

"Do you think he would be willing to talk with me?"

"I don't know. How would that work?"

"We'll use an old routine and have you doze off while I bring him out to talk with me. You can stay and sit in the corner and watch like we did when you and Ruth both talked to me. I'll call you if I need you."

Babe put her head back against the comfy chair and closed her eyes. Tucci spoke to her in monotone about being in a peaceful place watching the clouds. She quickly dozed.

"Rudy, I am a friend of Beulah and Ruth and have been helping them through tough times. I've gotten to know them pretty well. I'd like to get to know you as well, so I can continue to keep you all out of trouble. While they are sleeping, I'd like you to come out and talk with me. There's nothing to be afraid of."

"What makes you think I'm afraid of you? You can't make me do anything I don't want to."

"Thanks for showing up, Rudy. I'd like to introduce my partner Sam."

"What do you mean? He's just a dog."

"He's my co-therapist, my helper. He's friendly. He's harmless. See, he's wagging his tail hoping you'll pet him."

"What did you want to talk to me about?"

"Well, first of all, how old are you? You act like you're about fourteen."

"I'm sixteen! Why do you want to know?"

"I just like to know how grown up someone is when I'm talking to them. You look quite a bit older than sixteen."

"How old do I look to you?"

"Oh, I'd say about thirty or thereabouts. What do you think, Sam?" nodding to the dog, who makes some low dog noises in his throat. "Sam thinks so too. See how he wags his tail?"

"What the hell does a dog know?"

"More than you think. He's telling me you remind him of Rip VanWinkle."

"Rip and wrinkle? What the hell are you talking about?"

"Rip VanWinkle was an old story about a man who fell asleep for twenty years and woke up older but didn't realize it. Sam says you remind him of that guy. You look much older than sixteen."

"You're weird, old man. Talking to a dog, telling weird stories. I thought you were supposed to be a doctor helping us."

"You're right on both counts. I can be weird and I'm a doctor. Right now, I'm going to do both and help you by having you fall asleep, but unlike the man in the story, instead of not realizing how much you've aged, after you wake up, you're going to know how much you have matured with age. The way we're going to have you sleep is another weird thing. I want you to sit and look at me, but don't blink. If you blink, you'll be tempted to blink again. After a certain number of blinks, you'll close your eyes and go to sleep. You won't know the number of blinks it takes to sleep, but I will. I may let you know, or I may just let it happen. While you sleep you will allow your brain to mature. For every minute you sleep here in my office, it will be like a year in your life. Now, I want you to look at me and not blink, and I will wake you when it's time."

Rudy stared at him. He tried to hold back, but within two minutes he blinked. He stared again. This blink took about a minute. After a third blink his chin went to his chest, and he was asleep. Tucci checked his watch, let him sleep for three minutes and woke him up.

"Did you get a good rest?"

"I slept pretty good."

"Still angry?"

"Not so much right now."

"I want you to go back to sleep for just a couple more minutes while I talk to you and Beulah."

Tucci reminded Rudy that his sleep from now on would be healing and would allow him to reach the maturity level he would have had if it had matched his true age. He would talk to him again in a few days and see how he was doing. He discussed it with Babe and they agreed to meet again in four days.

After they left, Tooch turned to his new-found companion, partner, co-therapist and scratched his ears. Thanks, buddy, that was a great help.

Chapter 35: Kraft and Cooper

Following up on the topaz earring clue, Kraft became much more focused on the late jeweler's romantic liaisons. As he plowed on, he found more evidence pointing to the woman in the photo with the earrings. It became clear that there was a falling out between her and the jeweler. It had not been the first time they had been at odds. There were two other screaming matches between them, witnessed by others, that Kraft knew about. In the searching of her apartment, another topaz earring was found. As the evidence accrued, Beulah appeared less likely to be involved in the crime itself, though she seemed to have a peculiar sensibility about the deed and the place where it occurred. As the evidence changed the focus, the uncanny clairvoyance or whatever it was that Beulah had was puzzling. He suggested to Cooper, in spite of how the evidence was piling up, to stay in touch with Beulah and the others and continue to learn what he could. Cooper didn't mind. There was an ambiance about these ladies that intrigued him. They were friendly and engaging but at the same time he picked up on a certain degree of reticence, especially from Lisa. All in all, though, they were fun.

After meeting with Kraft, Clark called Lisa and set up another get-together with the three ladies. The weather being nice, they agreed to meet at the park where there was a small walk-up coffee stand nearby. There were picnic benches where they could all sit and catch up some more. When the ladies arrived, Clark was sitting on one of the benches leaning back with his elbows on the bench looking up at a couple of squirrels bickering at each other in one of the trees.

Clark said, "Quite the chatter up there, isn't it?"

Lisa responded, "Are you warming up to a conversation with three ladies?"

Clark tipped his fedora and smiled. "Nice to see you again. I'm ready to hear all about the latest, and the old stuff. I always wondered how things turned out for others after I graduated and left for the marines."

After sitting at the picnic table exchanging stories for half an hour, Babe looked up and saw Tucci strolling down the path with Sam on a leash. She leaned over to Emily and said, "Look who's coming."

Tucci ambled down the path toward them carrying a plastic bag with dog poop in it. "Well hello ladies and sir. Beautiful day, isn't it?"

Emily spoke up. "Clark, this is doctor Tucci. Both Babe and I have been introduced to him in the past. Looks like you've got a new friend, Doctor, and this is Clark Cooper, and Lisa Barnes, old high school classmates."

"Meet my new partner, Sam. We adopted each other a little more than a week ago."

Clark reached out to shake his hand, but it was obviously occupied with the plastic bag, so he tipped his hat instead. "Hi, are you the John Tucci who has consulted with the police and the courts from time to time? You also served time in the military as a psychiatrist – on a missile base, I believe?"

"Sounds like you've been doing some research."

"No, Sir. Your reputation precedes you. I work for the state police, and I also spent some time in the military. I heard about you during some of the intelligence briefings from time to time."

Meanwhile, Sam was snuggling up to the ladies trying to get some petting and ear scratching, his bushy tail wagging. The ladies were happy to comply with his requests. Tucci sat with them while Sam soaked up the affection. He had proved to be a good companion, and Tucci was glad to see him getting plenty of attention.

Clark was intrigued with this man whom he had heard so much about.

"So, Doctor, what sort of work have you been doing lately? Anything with my friends in the state police?"

"No, just my general practice, and lately with my new co-therapist here. He keeps me company and provides me with excellent consultation."

They all chuckled at the notion.

"You do consult with my colleagues from time to time, though, don't you?"

"Rarely, any more. I must be careful in a community as small as ours about confidentiality. What I can consult about are cases that are basically theoretical. My services haven't been requested for some time now."

Emily piped in. "It's good to hear that, since two of us have had the good fortune to be his clients."

Lisa laughed. "Don't tell him which two. Let him guess."

They all giggled, and all three ladies jokingly pointed fingers at each other, shifting back and forth to keep Clark in the dark. Then Lisa changed the subject. "What are you working on these days, Clark?"

Babe piped in, "Do you happen to be working with Detective Kraft? He and I have had some conversations about a murder up in Pierce County where I had done some birdwatching and had some eerie experiences"

"Well, I can't talk about police work that is ongoing. Right now, I'm just trying to catch up with a bunch of old classmates and catch up on old times."

After sitting for a few minutes, Tucci stood up and Sam jumped to his feet. "I'd better be off to find a receptacle for this poop bag. Got some work to do back at the office. It's been nice to meet you all. I won't spoil the puzzle about which two of you I have met before. Nice to meet the other two of you. Let's go,

Sam."

As they watched Tucci meander away, Clark smiled and said, "The man was quite an enigma in the military before he left. He had an uncanny way of interviewing people who were facing serious charges. You ladies are lucky you found him."

Chapter 36: Maturation

About a week later, Babe had her next appointment with Tucci. During that week, Babe had been called by Kraft, telling her that the person who had killed the jeweler had been arrested and confessed to the crime. It was the lady who lost her topaz earring. Babe was off the hook from the policeman's perspective. He wanted her to know that. Cooper was assigned to another case in another part of the state, much to the chagrin of all the ladies. Babe was still perplexed with how to deal with her husband's death. Tucci looked at her and asked, "How are you and Ruth getting along?"

"Seemingly well. Occasionally we talk something over in my dreams at night. We seem to be in agreement about most things after looking at several sides of an issue. I don't seem to be having any daytime dreams anymore."

"What are some of the issues that you talk about?"

"Oh, a variety of things like whether or not to take a painting class, whether or not to try watercolor, other mundane things. We struggle about what to do with John's stuff. He has books, a gun, clothes, and there's always his cane."

"What are your thoughts together about his cane?"

"We're perplexed. It is something that was used in a crime, but it was years ago, and both John and Eddie are gone. Why bring up something that will just stir up pain and discomfort? We generally just put the decision aside like we put the cane aside. We decided to leave it with you."

"How are you getting along with Rudy?"

"I haven't heard from him. Is he still asleep?"

"I'm not sure. Shall I call him out and see?"

Babe nods and lowers her chin to her chest and closes her eyes. When they open, her demeanor changes. A smile erupts.

"Good to see you again, Doc. You have quite a knack for helping a guy relax."

"Are you getting along better with the others now?"

"Like that Rip guy that you mentioned, I got some good rest, and it helped me to cool my temper and get a lot more mellow in my approach to people. I think it'll help me to get what I want much better than fighting does. Thank you for helping. See, even thanking you gets me more mileage."

"Are you staying out of trouble?"

"No longer an issue for me, Doc. I'm older now and mellow as jello. The ladies and I generally see eye to eye on most things."

They chatted for a few minutes and Tucci asked to see Babe again.

When she came out, she said, "Doc, remember when you thought about toning down our visits and stretching them out a bit? It was too early for me to do that, but things have changed. I'm going to art classes twice a week. I joined Emily and her friends in a book club that meets bi-monthly. I'm out for coffee with a few friends once or twice a week. Maybe I'm ready to stretch out our visits a bit. I don't want to stop. I just think I'm ready to try a bit more on my own."

Tucci looked at her and smiled. "As always, I am cueing off of you. I think you are absolutely right. I am going to be gone for about ten days. Let's schedule again in three weeks and see how it goes."

It was the beginning of a series of pauses. They expanded the interims. There were only minor bounces. After about a year, they went to 'pro re nata' – as needed.

Chapter 37: Tucci's Ending

Several years had passed. John Tucci was now in his seventies. He was in the hospital, but in the hospice section. His diagnosis was pancreatic cancer. The disease sneaked up on him and was not treatable. It progressed rapidly, but the hospital staff seemed to be able to keep him comfortable. His two daughters had managed to arrive from out of state to offer some comfort. Babe, Lisa and Emily were allowed to visit together, but the visit had to be time-limited to avoid wearing him out too rapidly. Emily and Babe had to fight back tears. Lisa held his hand.

"Thank you for being a friend and helper to both of my best friends, John. You've done more than I could imagine to change their lives for the better, and believe me, it's made an impact on my life as well.

"Well, Lisa, working with your friends has made my life better as well. Looking back, I only have a couple of regrets in my life. The first is that I didn't join the drama club in high school when I had the chance. The second is that I didn't take piano lessons or learn Spanish. You never know how life would have been sweeter, having done those things. Other than that, I've had a pretty good life, a good wife, and I've been blessed to end up helping people."

All three ladies had to giggle when they heard his regrets. Leave it to "The Tooch" to ease the situation and change the perspective.

He looked at Babe and said, "By the way, I hope you don't mind. When I knew my time was limited, I assumed it would be OK to find a suitable place for the special cane that you left in my possession, so I donated it to the local historical museum as an unusual artifact. They were more than pleased with the gift."

It wasn't long after that when the nurse asked the ladies if they had one last thing to say to him before they had to leave.

Emily tearfully kissed him on the cheek, and said, "Goodbye and thank you, Doctor." Babe kissed his hand and squeezed it. Lisa kissed her hand and touched it to his forehead. "Bon voyage, Doctor."

They found out that he had passed that night.

Several months later, a rather large package arrived unexpectedly at Babe's house. It had come from an attorney's office. Attached to it was a letter from the attorney addressed to Beulah Blanche.

"Dear Ms. Blanche,

I represent Dr. John Tucci who recently passed away. In his will, he bequeathed two paintings to you that he was sure that you would appreciate. One is an original work of art. He suggests that you have it appraised."

Babe opened the package. In it were the Monet print that hung in his office, as well as the painting that she had given to him. A note from Tucci was attached.

"Babe,

Your change of style from the abstract to the soft gentleness of your scene reflects to me the healing process you are undergoing. You've gone from Beulah to Babe and unlike me, you are not yet destined for an alternative world, so I hope you continue to enjoy the one you are in, and I hope that the salamanders continue to be peaceful. Take as much pleasure in these paintings as I have.

Your friend, John"

She wiped her tears. "Thanks, Tooch. Because of you the salamanders are getting along quite well."

End

WORKING WITH KIDS

As a child psychiatrist, I often found it necessary to attend to many aspects of the family. After all, kids need parents, school, other kids, other doctors, and everything works together. One day while attending to custody matters of a family in a court setting, I happened to run into a friend who also happened to be a lawyer.

"Hi, Bob. Congratulations! I heard your wife recently gave birth to another baby. How are she and the baby doing?"

"Well, she's healthy and so is the baby."

He looked a bit worn and rather perplexed.

"Is everything OK?"

Bob did a funny upturn of his mouth and said, "I'm not sure."

"OK," I said, "What's up?"

"Well, we have another son who is five years old, and we thought he was happy about having a new brother on the way. He is in kindergarten and doing well there. He gets along with other kids and works well with the teacher, but as Mary was getting closer to having the baby, the teacher told us that he started to spend a lot of time sitting around and drawing pictures and not interacting much with her or the other kids, and this behavior has continued after the baby arrived. Mary is concerned about this and so am I. We especially got concerned when the teacher said that he draws all his pictures in black crayon. She advised us to get him to a counselor to see if he is distressed about having some competition in the family. I'm glad I bumped into you; can we work something out for you to see him?"

"Sure, Bob. I will tell my secretary to put you in to the quickest opening I have that fits for you. I can meet with you and your wife to get any personal family issues that might be important to consider, and then I can spend some time with your son. "

The visit was arranged. Bob and Mary spoke to me in a separate phone call for some background information prior to Bob bringing Robert Jr. to the appointment. I met them in my office waiting room, shook hands with Bob, then reached down and shook the boy's hand and said, "Hello, Robert, I am glad to meet you. I am a friend of your dad's. He told me that you are quite the artist."

The boy looked up at me and said, "Hi. My daddy says you are a nice man who likes to play with kids and talk to them."

"Well, Robert, your father is right. What kinds of things do you like to play?"

"I like to play make believe." He smiled with a sparkle in his eye.

"Well, imagine that, so do I. What do you like to make believe about?"

"I like to make believe I'm on an adventure."

"Do you like to adventure alone or with someone else."

"Well, if you like to adventure, too, you can come with me. We could go hunt for hidden treasure."

"I've got an idea. Why don't we go into my office, and we can go for an adventure using paper and color crayons. That way we can go wherever we want to go without taking a bus. I have some crayons and paper right here in my office."

"That's a good idea. I like to draw, and I love crayons. Do you drive a bus?"

"No, Robert, I just meant that we could do an adventure by using make-believe, and we wouldn't have to leave your daddy here while we go. He can wait for us out here while we do our adventure."

We entered the office, and I got out the supplies and set them up at a small kid-size table for him. We both sat in kid-size chairs. He got the crayons out of the box and grabbed the black crayon. He started to draw a couple of stick men and said, "This one is me and that one is you. We're digging for treasure." He drew what was probably a shovel in the hand of one of the figures, and a black sort of blob that the other seemed to reach for on the ground.

He grinned at me and said, "We found the treasure." The whole picture was in black crayon.

I said, "Boy you sure like the color black, don't you."

He looked up at me with a twinkling smile and said, "Yes, black is my favorite color. It's the same color as licorice and that's my favorite candy! When my new brother gets big enough, we're going to go on a treasure hunt for licorice just like we are doing now. I can hardly wait."

I looked at him and said, "You know what? I just happen to have some treasure over there in my desk drawer, but you will have to ask your dad if you can have it now or wait until after you have your dinner."

We talked about different types of licorice for several minutes, sugar-coated, Good & Plenty, salted stars, black laces, Australian black, --- you name it. Then we talked about his excitement to have a brother.

"He's too small to play with now, but when he grows bigger, we're gonna be buddies and go adventuring together."

I reassured Bob that black was not the color of depression. For this little boy, it was the color of excitement.

Make up your mind

My first appointment of the day was with a gentleman of around sixty-five years and about two day's growth of salt and pepper beard. He had worked in a lumber mill most of his life, and I could still see the callouses of his hands.

After introductions and my inquiries about what brought him to see me, he said, "I am the grandfather of a fifteen-year-old boy who has been living with me for the past several years. Custody was awarded to me because of his mother's drug and alcohol problems. His father is not in the picture, having left his family some years ago and moving out of state to parts unknown. Since hitting his teen years, this lad has become more of a handful, not wanting to follow my directions, and arguing about every little thing. I made the appointment with you to see if you could help."

"Is the mother in the picture at all?"

"She lives in town, is remarried, and has been through AA, and, as far as I can tell, has been clean and sober for about eighteen months. However, her personality has not changed much, and she tends to be a flake. She would not be a very reliable parent. She calls him about once a week and talks to him for about five minutes, and that's about it."

Arrangements were made for me to see the boy the following week.

When the teen arrived, he was heavy set with disheveled hair and dressed in clothes that had seen a lot of wear. He came sullenly into the office, plopped down in a chair next to my desk, and said, "You can't make me take any medicine. I'm not taking any and you can't make me."

I looked into his frown and said, "You can't trick me into giving you any medicine. I wouldn't give you any medicine even if your grandfather paid me to give it to you."

He scowled at me but looked puzzled. "Well, that's what doctors do, isn't it? If kids aren't behaving right, they get pills, right?"

"Wrong! I'm the one who decides about who gets medicine and who doesn't, and you're not getting pills just because you want them. Kids need to be helped with what they can do to make it work out better for themselves without using drugs. Why don't we start out by telling me what is making you so angry, so we can help you to fix it without pills. We'll just talk."

"You mean I was brought here just to talk? What a waste of time."

"Well, not really a waste of time. You get to cool off some of the tension at home by being here. You get to complain about things that bother you without being called on the carpet for doing so, and you get to get even with your grandfather by costing him money to bring you here. Not bad for an hour's work."

"But I don't want to live with my grampa. I want to go back to live with my mom."

"Well, so far, what you're doing to make that happen isn't working so well, is it? Why don't we do it my way for a while. Coming here to talk will cool things off at grampa's house, and you can bitch all you want to and not worry about my snitching. I can tell him that we agreed to continue to meet and talk, and that he can lighten up a bit and let me work with you. Maybe eventually we can work something out between grampa and mom. Meanwhile, maybe we should start out on the right foot by introducing ourselves to each other. My name is Jerry, but in this place, I go by Dr. V."

"My name is Georgie Jensen." He paused, looking befuddled. "You're never going to work out things with my grampa and mom. He's a stubborn, grumpy old guy and he doesn't like my mom very much. He is set in his ways."

"Well, like I said, your way isn't working so well. Want to give my way a shot?"

"So, we meet once a week and talk, and that's it?"

"Not exactly. To make it work, you've got to make it look like it's working. You'll have to ease up on your grumpy behavior at home and follow directions, so grampa thinks that talking to me is working, and he can back off and not feel like he's got to ride you. Ease off the attitude in school, do your homework, and smile once in a while. You do your part of the work; I'll work on grampa, but it'll take a little time."

Georgie stared at me for a few moments. Then he began to smile. "That might just work. Okay, I'm up for that. Let's start talking."

We met weekly for about two months. The friction eased at home. I tapered the meetings down to every two weeks for a while, then once a month. The end of the school year was approaching. Georgie continued to ask about living with his mother. I told him I planned to have a conversation with his grampa to see what we could work out during the summer.

"That won't do anything. He won't give in to letting me live with her."

"I'm not talking about full-time living with her. I'm talking about working on visits for starters, but you've got to set it up so it can work."

"Set it up how?"

"Let me give you an example. Say you want to visit her for several days around her birthday, so you approach your grampa about two weeks before and tell him you would like to visit her, and to show him that you can make it work well. You want him to watch how you behave for the next two weeks to see that he can trust you. Then you do everything he wants you to do and a few extras around the house, but you make sure he notices."

"Well, he hardly ever notices anything I do unless it's a problem."

"Well, that's why you bring his attention to what you're going to do before you do it, so he's sure to notice."

"Oh, I get it. Make sure he knows it before I do it."

"You're catching on. Have things toned down at home since we started this? How about school?"

"Well, so far I'm passing all my classes, and I haven't been grounded for anything."

"Looks like you've been keeping your end of our bargain with me. Ready for me to jump into this plan with grampa?"

"Well, so far what you're telling me seems to be helping."

I called the grandfather that evening.

———

"Mr. Bridger, just another check-in about Georgie. He says he is doing better at school and keeping out of trouble at home. He wants to have a sit-down with you and talk some about his mother. I think he's ready, and I would encourage you to do that with him. I think you'll be surprised, and I think it might be a good idea, if you are so disposed, to seriously consider what he is about to ask you. I'm giving you a heads up because he wants to spend a few days with his mother."

Grandfather Bridger did not seem to be taken by surprise. "Whatever you have been doing with that kid is working well. I am more than happy to follow your lead. Thank you so much. I'll look forward to whatever you suggest."

"Just listen to his pitch, Mr. Bridger. If you have any questions, just give me a call. Thanks."

I had another visit with Georgie scheduled for the week after his planned conversation with grampa.

"I can't believe you pulled it off, Doc. He listened to your plan and let me go. It was a great weekend."

"You underestimated yourself, Georgie. You are the one who pulled it off. It's how you held yourself together over time that worked."

Summer was coming along, so it was a good time for Georgie to be able to spend more time with his mom. We were able to work out an arrangement to have Georgie spend alternate weeks at his mother's home and at grampa's house. He continued to see me once a month. In July, he said, "Doc, maybe we should look again at whether or not I should be taking some medication."

"What's up, Georgie?"

"I'm just not feeling as good as I thought I would."

"Things going OK with your mom?"

"It's alright, but she doesn't always seem to even know that I'm there. She's busy with other things. She doesn't track me like grampa does. Sometimes it feels like she doesn't really care. We don't really talk much. When I'm at grampa's, he and I have gotten to where we can actually sit down and have a conversation."

"Are you able to connect with friends since school has let out?"

"I don't have a lot of friends. I have a few people that I saw at school."

"Have you ever thought about getting involved in sports? Sometimes that's a good way to start connecting, at least with other guys. I don't think we need to start looking at pills yet. Does your grampa have hobbies that he could teach you? Does he fish? Does he build things? Does he have things that he could do with you?"

A month later, when we again met, Georgie told me he had signed up to play high school football. He had spent time talking to his grandfather over the past month, learning a lot about him that he had not known. His respect for the older gentleman had grown. He looked at me and said, "Doc, I really appreciate all your help in getting me to be able to live with my mom and get to know her, but I really think that what I want to do is to live with my grandfather and visit my mom just once in a while."

"Georgie, I am glad that you were able to sort that all out by trying things out and using that good brain of yours, that you didn't always remember was there."

He looked at me and grinned.

Our next visit was a month out. He was living full-time with grampa and seeing his mom for breakfast on occasional Sundays. Football practice and getting together with friends took a lot of his time, so we agreed to get together again in three months. When that appointment came up, it was cancelled. About two weeks later, Georgie called me and left a message, "Doc, you helped me a lot, but I don't think I need to come in anymore. I learned some helpful stuff from you, but now I think I can remember to use 'that good brain of mine' on my own. Thanks. See you around."

I smiled on hearing the message and thought, "He's gonna be OK. He knows where I am if he needs me."

Star-crossed

A new patient had arrived, and it was time to see him for the initial exam. It was my first month as a new resident, and one of my jobs was to see the new arrivals for the initial interview and physical exam. The new patient, Lester P, was in his twenties, 5 feet, 7inches tall, and about 180 lbs. He was admitted to the hospital on a police mental health hold. Apparently, he had been charged with stalking a co-ed and resisting orders to cease and desist. Ultimately, he was arrested, and the court considered him to be mentally ill, resulting in his ending up here. As he was escorted into the examining room by Nurse Whit, he reached out to shake my hand, he said, "How do you do, Doc. I'm Lester, and I've got quite a story to tell you."

I reached out to shake his hand and said, "I am sure you do, Lester. Have a seat, and you can tell me all about it. I will also be doing a physical exam today, so when we're finished talking, I'll need to listen to your heart and lungs and check you over."

Lester started right in. "I'm so glad I have someone who will listen to me about what happened. It was glorious! I'm in love with my star-crossed soulmate, Doc. Let me tell you about it. No one else, including the police, seems to want to listen, but it's so real!"

He went on to relate how he, as a college student, had attended a class in astronomy. It was not his major, but he needed the credits. The class required several late evening sojourns to scan the evening sky. Lester described himself as not a very socially inclined person, so in this setting, with both men and women students, the mixture of social interactions was a bit unnerving to him. One particular coed was friendly and helpful to him. He tended to hang close to her as the class leader lectured about the star formations. At one point as they sat on a knoll to watch a meteor shower, a particularly bright meteor lit up the sky, and Lester was astounded.

"I was star-struck. She was right next to me. We felt it together. It was clear. We were star-struck lovers. We were destined to be together forever. It was a new beginning for both of us."

As the story went on, it became clear to me that Lester's vivid perception of that moment was not the same as that of the girl. The hospital had access to the police reports, which I had perused before the interview. Lester had pursued her relentlessly, but she became more wary and fearful of him, and eventually obtained a stalking order.

"Do you understand how it is that you ended up here in the hospital, Lester?"

"It's all a misunderstanding, Doc. It was an encounter written in the stars. We were meant to be."

"Do you see where all of this attention coming to her at such a fast pace might have been a bit overwhelming to her?"

"It overwhelmed me too, Doc. That's what made it so real and so captivating. I don't see how she could have missed the implications."

"The implications?"

"That we would become immortal, one with the universe, and that we would live a world of bliss."

"And why were you picked from among the multitudes to have this experience?"

"Well, some others may have been picked as well. I just don't have that information. I just know that I was selected in a special way to have this ecstatic experience, and I don't want to waste it."

"You realize, don't you, Lester, that the result of this experience and your reaction to it has caused numerous people to think you were having a mental illness, and that's why you ended up here in the hospital?"

"They'll come around, Doc. Now that I've found this in my life, I need to keep it. Look in my eyes. Can't you see the mystical glow emanating from them?"

"Many wise people would see this kind of feeling and thinking as delusional. It could complicate your life a great deal."

"But, Doc, without this in my life, my whole purpose would be shattered. I would just be a nobody."

Lester remained on a high note throughout the rest of the exam. He would remain on the unit throughout the remainder of my six months rotation there. He tended to focus on eyes. He would comment on what he saw in other people's eyes as though he could read their thoughts. He researched what it would take to become an optometrist. He continually asked for permission to get a telescope to look at the stars. Medications tended to slow him physically but didn't appear to alter his magical thinking process. Periodically I would remind him that most people would not see the world in the same way, but he would remind me that it was exactly what made him so special and that without the impact that the star had made on him, his purpose in life would be futile. His life history demonstrated his sense of isolation. He had lost his parents to drugs and was raised in several foster homes. He scraped by in school and managed to get a grant to attend college, but his sense of aloneness was evident.

When I left that rotation to go to another hospital, I lost track of Lester for a while. I never forgot him and often wondered about him. I saw his need to hang on to something meaningful in his life in many of my subsequent patients. It somehow helped me to understand them better and to perhaps help them.

I ran into Lester a number of years later in the most unlikely way. While filling in for a short time for a colleague at a drug rehab center, I entered a room with a group of patients and saw Lester. It didn't surprise me, though I was disappointed at seeing him there after all these years, until I discovered that he was there in the role of a staff person. That blew me away. After the meeting was over, I had the opportunity to speak with him.

"Lester, I am so delighted to see you after all these years. Obviously, you're in much better shape than when I last saw you."

"Doc, it's good to see you as well. You don't know how much you helped me. You listened to me. You were kind to me, and you said something to me that I couldn't shake out of my mind. You said, 'Lester, you have a need to connect with people, but it would help you to do so in a less magical way.' It was a simple statement, far from seismic, but its impact was surprising to me over time. I watched how you helped people, and it gave me some perspective on what it means to have a meaningful life. It helped me to gradually leave all that magical star-struck stuff behind for something real. I eventually trained as a paramedic and managed to get a job. Life is better now."

"I'm glad it turned out well for you. I want you to know that you taught me as well. I learned to be patient and to listen between the lines. It doesn't take a genius to be kind to people. Thank you, Lester."

As I have continued to practice this profession over the years, I have learned as much from my patients about human nature as anything they have learned from me. Thanks to all of you Lesters out there.

Rosco the Messiah

Rosco arrived at the psychiatric unit just after ten PM on a Saturday. I was on call. The cops who brought him skirted the ER and brought him directly for treatment on a police hold, Apparently, he had been in the local movie theater ranting and raving about saving souls. He had tested negative on a breathalyzer and resisted police efforts to remove him from the theater. Rosco was a man in his thirties, dressed in torn jeans and a plaid shirt with unruly hair. He was unshaven for several days and his hands were quite dirty. Within an hour, he was officially admitted to the unit, given some calming meds, showered, and given clean scrubs to wear. Once he was calmed and somewhat settled, I departed for the evening.

The following morning, I arrived on the unit to make rounds. Rosco was in the dayroom, engaging other patients in conversation, one after another, in excited and pressured tones. I quickly arranged to see him in my office, which was just off the dayroom. As a resident in training, the office was sparse with a metal desk and two chairs, an examining table, a bookshelf and a small window with a sturdy metallic screen. Rosco was brought in by an aide who closed the door behind him as he left.

"Rosco, I am Dr. V. My job is to get acquainted with you and try to understand how you got here to the hospital and how I might be able to help you."

"Doc, this is all a mistake. I don't belong here. I am just trying to save souls. People don't understand. I am the new messiah. I am Jesus reincarnated."

"Well, that's exactly why I'm here – to try to understand better how this came to be."

"Doc, the world is coming apart and Jesus saw that and came

back again. He became me to help save the world. I am just trying to let people know what we need to do."

"Well, how's that working out, Rosco? Are people listening?"

He looked at me, rather puzzled. "Well, not really, so far. Mostly, they just walk away."

"Maybe it's your approach. People often don't want to listen to advice from other people. It works much better if they think they thought of it themselves, and it was their idea."

I went on to do the normal physical exam and gather family and social information. He was a man who had been adopted as a baby and was brought up with two other adopted siblings in a middle-class family of hard workers.

After a week, Rosco was still trying to engage fellow patients with continuing appeals to listen to his preaching and advice, to the annoyance of many of them. I felt the need to somehow intervene to prevent some outbreak of physical tumult, so I sat down for another conversation with him.

"Well, Rosco, it looks like things are not going so well with your approach to other people here. Did you forget about helping people to come up with their own ideas to better their lives? Let's look at how Jesus did it. You're supposed to be stepping in for him, after all. Jesus didn't go around preaching to people. He just did his thing and let people follow his lead. He'd do a miracle and then talk to them. He would show them how to live their lives by example, not by ordering them to change."

"But, Doc, I've got to get their attention."

"Do it by being nice to them, not by yelling at them. Do it with kindness."

Rosco nodded and seemed to take it in.

"By the way, Rosco, I understand that you know something about carpentry. Your father, Joseph, was a carpenter, right? There happens to be an opening at the hospital carpentry shop, and with your experience, I would like to have you go there to help out. I think you would fit in nicely."

After another week, I went to the carpentry shop to check on how he was doing. He was busy sanding the top of a dresser.

"So, what do you think, Rosco? Are you doing better here with more things to do? You look a lot busier than you were on the unit."

"Doc, they just want to keep me working here. I've been mostly sanding the tops of things that other people are building. No one wants to talk about saving their souls."

"You seem to be doing a good job of sanding the furniture. Maybe they are working to follow your example to do what they can to save their souls without just talking about it. Maybe not pestering them about their salvation is a way that they can get on with their lives and learn to respect themselves and others."

Rosco continued working at the hospital carpentry shop. He had been legally committed to the hospital because the movie theater people had pressed charges against him, and the judge did not want to put him in jail when he obviously needed psychiatric care. After six months, he was released from his committment to outpatient treatment. I ran into him about a year later in the grocery store. He had a big smile on his face when he saw me.

"Doc, it's good to see you. I want to thank you for teaching me the best line of my life."

"What's that, Rosco?"

"Watch what I do, not what I say."

"I don't remember ever saying that to you."

"You didn't use those words, Doc, but it's what you taught me, and it stuck. You didn't tell me outright what to do, but let me figure it out for myself, and it worked. Now I'm out, working a job at the post office, and I have a lady friend. My life is on track again, and I want to thank you for being who you are, so I could see who I could be."

I wished him well and we shook hands. I have not run into him since.

Awakening:

I was in my early forties when I was scheduled to see a woman in her late fifties who was married to a prominent businessman in the area. She entered the office with perfectly coiffed hair that was brown with streaks of gray and was wearing a yellow pants suit. She was about five-foot-nine and wore shoes without heels. She was sparse with her makeup. She reached out her hand to shake mine and said,

"Hello, Dr. Tucci, my name is Elaine Gorse. I thought I should make an appointment with you to help me look at some of the potential changes coming in my life."

I shook her hand. Her grip was firm, but soft. "I'm happy to meet you, Elaine. I guess you should have a seat. It appears you are all set to get right down to business."

I had a small office with a settee, a desk, and a couple of chairs. Two diplomas hung inconspicuously in a corner of the opposite wall. She sat in the settee and spread herself out just a little. She seemed both excited and relaxed.

"I don't think we have met, but I met your wife briefly at the market. She was introduced to me by a friend. She struck me as a very pretty and pleasant woman. I heard about you from another friend who has had the opportunity to see you professionally, but I won't get into that. You may have heard of my husband. He is a well-known businessman in this area, and he is part of the reason I am here. We have been married for over thirty years and have raised three children, who are now raising their own families. Frankly, Doctor, I am a bit bored with my life."

"Do you see your kids or grandkids much?"

"One lives out of state; the other two in other parts of the state. We see them from time to time. Sometimes we baby sit their kids for several days at a time." Her affect was rather flat as she spoke about them.

"So, if you are bored, what kind of hobbies or interests do you have?"

"After the kids grew up and moved out, I took up painting for a while. I took lessons from a local artist, from several local artists, but the art never really embedded itself in me. I thought about taking up the violin, but at my age, I would probably be better off taking up the drums. I joined this women's group and that one, but there was no excitement. My husband, John, was always busy with his business. We'd go to the symphony, the theater, the ballet. It helped, but something was missing, or it really was never there. I didn't realize it until I met someone, but now that I brought it up, I find myself a little hesitant to go on about it. I just keep blathering on and I'm not allowing you to ask what you need to know about me."

"What you say you're blathering about is what I need to know about you. That's the actual reason that you came here to talk with me, isn't it?"

She smiled knowingly at me. With some brief hesitation, she went on.

"You're a bit younger than I. So is the man I am about to tell you about. It's one of the reasons I decided to come to you rather than an older psychiatrist who's been around this town a bit longer. In fact, both you and the other man I'm talking about, are a breath of fresh air in my life finally."

She waited for me to start my query.

I quietly sat and waited for her to continue talking.

"Don't you want to know more?"

"You're going to tell me, aren't you?"

She looked at me for a moment. "Aren't you going to ask me questions?"

"No need, it's your story. Tell me about it, and if I have any questions, I'll ask you then."

"Well, aren't you the smart one!"

By this time, she was sitting upright on the settee. She looked as though she might bounce up and walk out.

I looked at her and said, "My first question to you is, would you like a drink of water. You look a little dry in the mouth." I got up and opened the small refrigerator behind my desk and took out a bottle. "It's flavored, but no calories. Would you like berry or lemon?"

"Lemon, please." She couldn't seem to help but smile.

"That's fortunate. That's what I've got left."

"Do you have a glass?"

"Sorry, you'll have to drink from the bottle. I forgot to get cups."

Elaine couldn't help but stifle a chuckle as she leaned back into the settee. "My friend was right. You seem to be a no-nonsense kind of person. And she was probably right when she said that was exactly what I probably needed."

"Exactly or probably?"

"Yes, exactly <u>was</u> the correct word."

"Okay, you made the decision to be here. So why don't we start by telling me what you're dealing with, and hopefully I can help you through the process of sorting it out, so you can make whatever decisions you need to make. Let's start with your telling me when the boredom started."

Elaine put her feet under her legs on the settee. She made herself comfortable as she prepared to get underway.

"I think I began to get bored shortly after our honeymoon. We were not rich at the time, but our parents managed to put together enough money to send us to Seattle for a few days. We saw the sights – Pike Place Market, the Space Needle, and whatever we could find, and we spent a lot of time in the bedroom. When we got home to Eugene, things settled down more to the daily grind of running a business. Days were long at the store. Nights were better. I liked the sex. However, I was soon pregnant, and not long after that, the honeymoon was definitely over."

"Tell me about your husband, John. What did you like about him that made you want to marry him?"

"He made me laugh. He had a droll sense of humor. He was sweet and kind, not just to me, but to most people. He is really a good guy and a good companion, but he's always very busy. It's work, work, work, and even when we took time off for vacations, he was on the phone. Life for me became whatever I made life for me to be. Once the kids grew up, I found myself fending for myself. At least that's how it felt to me. It felt as though I had lost my purpose in life. I realized that I was bored."

"Did something change for you?"

She smiled and seemed to brighten up. It was as though I had pulled the plug and allowed her feelings to flow out.

"Yes, I met someone. It was a coincidence, but for some reason, it felt like a happy one. He was about ten years younger than I am. I literally bumped into him while in line at a coffee shop and spilled his coffee on him. I offered to get him a fresh cup. We sat down together to clean him up and ended up chatting together for the next hour or so. I guess I was a bit taken with him and ripe for something fresh. Maybe he was too, because we exchanged information, and agreed to meet again for coffee sometime. Sometime came and went, but he kept popping into my head. About six weeks later, when my husband called about three in the afternoon to say he would be working late and would not be home for the dinner date we had planned, I picked up the phone and called my new friend. Before I knew it, our new 'friendship' was off and running."

"How long ago did this new relationship start?"

"About a year and a half ago."

"And -------?"

"I am needing to sort out for myself, where I go from here. That's why I'm here, hoping you can help me think it through."

"Are you here to solidify what you have already decided? Or are you wanting me to help you change your mind? Or neither?"

"Doc, some of my friends picked up on my boredom and thought I was depressed. That's how I got your name, but I don't think I need antidepressant medicine. I need someone to talk to. Saying my thoughts out loud helps me to hear them more clearly and to think them through instead of just mulling them around in my head. Talking helps me to separate my thoughts from my feelings. I don't have anyone else that I trust enough to talk this over with. I am hoping I can do this with you."

"Elaine, you're right on about the talking and sorting process. I'll do my best to help you do that. Ultimately the decisions will be yours. Let's start by telling me more about this new person and how he seems to fill the gaps in your life. I need to know a bit more."

"Okay, he's married, but they are separated and probably headed for the divorce court. He has two teen-age kids, both boys, that really idealize him. He's a teacher, and a pretty good one from what I hear. He and I hit it off well. We meet on the sly, but we have similar interests."

"Have you been intimate?"

"You cut right to the chase, don't you, Doc?"

"To use your own words, I don't want to have to chase you. I don't need details, but if you are in bed together, it's part of the equation."

"Yes, Doc, we've worked out some arrangements. He says he enjoys sex with me much more than with her."

"And you?"

"Yes, Doc, it's quite good. It's been a long time since sex has been exciting."

"So, it sounds like you first need to see if he is really headed to a divorce. Then you also need to consider whether it's worth giving up the financial security of your present lifestyle. Or, --- there is also the option of continuing to carry on the affair. Clearly there are ramifications with whatever you decide."

"That's a very succinct evaluation of my circumstances, Doc."

"Well, it's a good starting point. I'm sure you can build on the rest. Talking it over will probably help you to look long and hard at the consequences of whatever decisions you make. That's what this is all about, right?"

"That's what I meant about just mulling it over in my head. It's more about feelings and not about the reality of circumstances. You have me thinking already, Doc."

"Can you tell me what you know about where this other fellow's marriage faltered for him? You've given me a sense about yours."

"Well, I presume that the romance just flattened out like it does with lots of partners after you get to know them pretty well and can predict what they are going to say or do."

"Some people think that it makes them more consistent and reliable. It's sometimes a matter of perspective. Sounds like the two of you haven't talked a lot about details with your partners, but more in general."

"It's strange, Doc, but you're right. It's almost as though that's too private to talk about, like an invasion of their privacy."

"Like your intimacy with John is really not his business?"

"Exactly. I hadn't thought about it that way until just now."

"So, it looks like there are still some feelings of caring about John."

"Yes, clearly there are."

We continued to talk in this vein for the rest of the hour, exploring her feelings and how they fit into her need for adventure, but also about how she felt she had lost that with John.

As we wound up the session, she appeared to be tired but spirited. We arranged to meet weekly for a while, with enough time between visits to digest it all. She said, "Thanks, Doc. I think this is what I needed."

We met weekly, as planned. We discussed her potential plans, her fears, her sadness at potentially leaving John, her thrills in the new-found excitement, and her concerns about telling her kids. Her new-found love affair was still on the sly, but she didn't know how long she could keep it up in this surreptitious manner.

We had been meeting about three months, and she said, "It's been some time now, Doc, and I've been able to sort a lot of things out, but it comes down to judging between my head and my heart. Do I choose my feelings or my thoughts? I don't want to hurt John, but my real excitement in life is in the other direction. You have been very useful in helping me to sort out my choices, but we have gone over and over those choices, and it's still the decision making that is mine alone. I've decided to take a break as far as our meetings go to let all these notions incubate for now if that's all right with you."

"I am here to help you make your own decisions. Looks like this is one you need to make. I'll take you off our weekly schedule, but you know we can meet again if you need to come in and sort some more."

It was about two weeks later when we got a call from Elaine, asking for an appointment. My secretary managed to get her in within a few days.

She arrived in her usual pants suit and with her coiffed hair. Her demeanor was subdued. She quietly entered the office and settled on the settee. I waited for her to talk to me. She was slow at doing so. She finally said, "John had a stroke about a week after our last appointment. It was severe. It took two days for him to come out of his coma. He is still in the hospital but is scheduled for rehab. He is aware of me and of his surroundings, but it will take a while to recover, and maybe only partially. I can tell that he is grateful that I am here. I am realizing how much I love the old boring guy, in spite of my exciting fling. The distraction was fun while it lasted. I see it now for what it was, and I'm glad that I had it, but real life goes on, and I'm strangely looking forward to spending more time, real time, with John."

I sat quietly with her as her eyes glistened with the tears that she tried to blink away. I sat down next to her on the settee and reached out to hold her hand.

She looked at me and smiled through her tears. "Doc, I came here to thank you. The opportunity to sort out my feelings has been very helpful. I see now that what my friends saw as depression was right, and I was doing my best to take care of it myself, but the opportunity to put my thoughts and feelings into words helped to make more sense out of my life, and John's illness has helped to solidify my feelings about him in a better way."

We talked for the next hour about not isolating while caring for John, getting the help she might need, and continuing contact with her kids and with friends. Before she left, I reminded her that she could call or come in to see me at any time that she felt the need, or wanted the contact, or even if just to talk.

She said, "I already know that Doc." She gave me a warm hug and walked out of the office.

I happened to run into Elaine several months later at a social event. She was with friends. John was with her in a wheelchair. She appeared to be in good spirits. She noticed me and smiled but did not otherwise acknowledge me or introduce me to her friends. It was obvious that she had kept our previous liaison to herself. It was a different kind of intimacy and our little secret. I could not help but notice how her demeanor was glowing. She was clearly no longer depressed. She seemed to have found the purpose in her life that had been missing. She had no further need to call me. It felt good.

THE ARTIST IN ME:

As a young child, one's imagination takes hold. Listening to stories on the radio, drawing pictures, and playing pretend were all great adventures. We were like stem cells from which could take off and form any of the cells of the body that were needed. We could go off in any direction in our lives, depending on circumstances. If something happened to block one route, another would be open to travel. Such was the case for me in the third grade. I liked to draw pictures. As we followed the teacher's direction in our classroom one day, I was drawing a scene of a house. It had windows, a door, a fence, a tree, and some grass. My teacher happened to be looking over my shoulder. She pointed to the grass and asked, "What is that?" When I told her it was grass, she commented that grass doesn't usually look like that. I was crushed. My first thought was, "I must not be a very good artist." Like a good stem cell, my future proceeded in another direction. My itinerary would not head toward an artistic bent.

As I grew older, science became a direction for me. When I hit algebra, biology, chemistry, and physics, my route was taking shape. One of my biggest insights came in my high school biology class. My teacher could be a hardnosed woman. To get a decent grade in the class, one had to keep a notebook. Into the notebook a variety of assignments were required. One such assignment was to draw some pictures of birds from the text. It had to be a freehand drawing. After staring at the picture for a while, I finally attempted to make something that resembled the pictures in the book. When I finished, I was amazed at how closely my drawings resembled those in the text. I said to myself rather astoundedly, "I must not be such a bad artist after all." It was a revelation, but a little too late, from my perspective.

Closer to high school graduation, while perusing some information about potential college scholarships in the area of chemistry, the teacher who taught me both biology and chemistry happened to peer over my shoulder and asked what I was doing. When I told her I was pursuing information about chemistry studies, she said, "I thought you were going to be a doctor." We talked, and again the stem cell shifted. Before I knew it, I was bound for college as a premed.

Hunkering down to pursue a medical career didn't forward any artistic bent in me. I no longer had to keep a notebook or make drawings. I had to memorize a lot and spend long evenings in books. I could appreciate beauty in my surroundings but was often in a hurry. A couple of years into my college career, I began to tire of the pace. My "liberal college" required me to take courses in English and history, and I began to feel my "stem cells" pulling me in that direction. I took a liking for literature, drama, and philosophy. I began to find my artistic bent, but not in painting, drawing, or color manipulation. It was more in the direction of the pursuit of a variety of ideas, yet I also knew that science intrigued me. I knew that my path had been paved well enough that I should pursue medicine as a career, but also leave room for art and ideas.

When I managed to get accepted to medical school, I found that I had a lot of data and biological knowledge to inculcate. Students were exposed to a variety of medical pursuits as part of their learning. Rotations through various departments exposed us to learning a variety of information, as a good education should do. Most of us found interests in each of the departments as we experienced them, some more than others. When I rotated through my psychiatry assignment, intrigue set in. I was fascinated. How people thought about things could vary like roses and buttercups in a field of wildflowers. Talking to people about their innermost thoughts, and how they came to where they now were, was sometimes like viewing a painting of their soul. I found that art takes many forms, and the art of understanding and conversing can be one of them. I no longer take umbrage with my third grade teacher. Stem cells will direct themselves where they will.

END

Jerome Vergamini M.D. is a retired psychiatrist who was raised in northern Wisconsin, went to small colleges in Minnesota, and got his medical degree at the University of Wisconsin-Madison in 1965. He finished a one-year rotating internship at St. Joseph Hospital in Denver and returned to University Hospitals in Madison for a three-year residency in psychiatry.

In 1969, the Viet Nam war was continuing. Dr. Vergamini was called into the US Air Force and was assigned to a missile base in Montana. Two years later, when his service ended, he returned to northern Wisconsin to serve as medical director and administrator to a small mental health clinic. After two years an opportunity came up to return for more training as a child psychiatrist. After completing two more years of training, he accepted an opportunity to practice in Eugene, Oregon, where he lives and worked until his retirement in 2020, as the Coronavirus pandemic exploded.

His practice over the years has included consultation to the courts and to numerous residential and outpatient treatment programs for children and adolescents. He has served on the board of the Oregon Psychiatric Association and served as president of that organization for one year. He was chief of psychiatry at Sacred Heart Hospital for a one-year term.

Dr. Vergamini had been married to the same woman for 56 years, until her death in 2021. They have three grown children and two grandchildren. This is his third book. The first, *A Fieldguide to the American Teenager, A Survival Guide for Parents*, was published in 2016, with co-author Ray Miskimins Ph.D., his second, *Quimby's Quandry* was published in 2022.

www.ingramcontent.com/pod-product-compliance
Lightning Source LLC
Chambersburg PA
CBHW040534170726
48295CB00012B/458